A Remembrance of Flesh:
Book 2 of the In-Between

Rebecca M. Senese

Other Books by Rebecca M. Senese

The In-Between Series
Book 1: A Reluctance of Blood
*Book 3: A Retribution of Soul

The Night Killers

Wreck the Halls: 5 Christmas Horror Stories

Oh the Horror! 5 Horror Stories

Bad Ends: 5 Horror Stories

With a Bite: 5 Vampire Tales

The Color of Blood: The Chronicles of Richard Damon

Who Killed Santa? A Christmas / Mystery Novella

A Very Zombie Christmas

The Beginners Guide to the Recently Deceased

Daily Bread

*Forthcoming

A Remembrance of Flesh:

Book 2 of the In-Between

Rebecca M. Senese

Published 2013 by RFAR Publishing
Toronto, Canada
http://www.RFARPublishing.com

This is a work of fiction. All characters appearing in this work are fictitious. Any resemblance to real persons, living or dear is purely coincidental.

Trade paper edition designed by Rebecca M. Senese
in InDesign CS5.5

Electronic editions designed by Rebecca M. Senese

Cover design: Rebecca M. Senese
Image © ivankmit / Dreamstime.com
Interior Image © 100ker / DepositPhotos.com

ISBN: 978-1-927603-14-7

A Remembrance of Flesh:
Book 2 of the In-Between

Prologue

I f anyone had ever asked her, Alexa Hammond would have said she
never thought that vampires would dream. But no one ever asked
her because who would? What kind of question was that for the
sanity of everyday life, for the bright sunshine of days filled with
classes, homework, friends and family? But Alexa did not have those
days anymore, or any days as a matter of fact. Alexa lived only for the
night.

Alexa was now a vampire.

And as a vampire, she found it fascinating to discover that yes, she
could in fact dream. She didn't dream every day but when she did dream,
she remembered it, and every dream was a dream of her former life, a
life of days.

A life now gone.

Constantine, her sire, told her the dreams would fade in time, in a few
more decades, a mere blink of the eye. Whenever he spoke of time that
way, it made her laugh. After only a year as a vampire, she still measured
her new existence in single nights.

At first Constantine found her laughter annoying as if she was mocking him. But she assured him she was not, and when he realized that, he grew to like it and would regale her with stories of his life and times, as he called it. When they weren't hunting, he held court and she lounged at his feet, listening to his stories, marvelling at his confidence, his intelligence, and his complete awareness of his own desires. When he desired her, he let her know it and she indulged him and indulged herself. He was forceful, brazen, strong, and assured.

Nothing at all like the men in her former life.

Nothing at all like Sebastian.

Odd that she would think of him here, in a pub in England. He could have been like her, if only he'd let himself. If only he'd taken that final step, tasted blood, he could be with her now instead of one of those freaks.

Those In-Between.

Anger still stirred in her when she thought of him, resisting. He'd claimed to love her but he'd rejected her.

All because of some silly loyalty to being human.

But he wasn't anymore. Not exactly. He was more vampire than human. Just one little sip would tip the balance. Still he'd resisted.

She'd wanted to finish turning him, but she couldn't. Only Bianca, the renegade vampire from Constantine's clan, could finish it. She'd bitten him in the first place, in a brazen attempt to start her own clan, in direct defiance of Constantine. Now Sebastian's polluted blood was poisonous to any other vampire.

Even to Alexa.

She pushed the glass of beer around on the coaster. She never drank it. She just used a half pint in front of her as a prop as she sat in a corner booth in this little out of the way pub in London. It still gave her a thrill to know she was here. She'd always wanted to travel to Europe but had imagined it wouldn't happen until after she graduated. Here she was, a year early, and had traveled on a private plane to get here no less.

Yet another thing she liked about Constantine: he was a man who planned for the long term. Of course being a vampire gave him quite the advantage with the markets. He could afford to wait for decades for things to bounce back and had acquired quite a fortune in the meantime.

Definitely enough that he could have met her in a nicer place. And enough that he should have acquired a watch along the way so he wouldn't be late.

She shifted on the scuffed wooden chair, feeling her skirt ride up on her legs. From the widening eyes of the man sitting at the bar in front of her, she knew he'd spotted it too. Hmm, not much work for that one. All she'd have to do is give him a smile, maybe push her glasses up her nose. A suggestive tilt of the head, indicating the back door, and he'd be out there like a shot, waiting for her.

So easy, it almost took all the fun out of it.

Almost.

She shifted again in her seat, this time uncrossing and recrossing her legs, getting the maximum movement of her skirt up her thigh, when the door opened at the front of the pub. Without seeing, she smelled the musky scent of Constantine on the air currents. She immediately dismissed the man at the bar from her mind.

Time for play later; now she had to work.

She glanced up just as Constantine glided around the corner of the booth. He was tall, with black wavy hair and a neatly trimmed beard that framed his generous lips. The sharp contours of his face matched the sleekness of his body and she admired the way his dark shirt tugged just so over his shoulders and chest. He dressed and moved with an elegant sophistication beyond any man in the room.

Well beyond any man she'd ever met in her former life.

Miles beyond Sebastian and his mustard or ketchup stained t-shirts.

With one motion, Constantine grabbed hold of the chair opposite her and pulled it out, slipping onto it. Over his shoulder, she saw the man at the bar turn away, disappointment etched on his face.

The waitress came over, pad of paper at the ready. Her look of indifference faded into slack jawed compliance when Constantine tilted his head back at her.

"A pint of lager," he said. He gestured at Alexa. "Another?"

"I'm fine," she said.

"That's all," Constantine said. "Make sure we aren't disturbed."

"Yes." The waitress's voice had a faraway sound to it. She turned and walked away.

Constantine leaned across the table toward her. Alexa breathed in the smell of him, musky with a hint of blood and decay, the best smell she'd ever experienced.

"You need to learn to drink that," he said. "It's important sometimes to appear as one of them."

She wrinkled her nose, knowing he liked the pixie look it gave her. "I didn't much like it when I was alive."

"Then order what you did like," he said. "This is part of your training, Alexa."

She pursed her lips. Sometimes she got tired of all the 'training' crap. Why should vampires have training? Next thing she'd be getting homework.

The waitress returned, depositing a pint in front of Constantine. He waved her away without looking at her. Confusion crossed the woman's face and then she wandered off, almost bumping into a table.

"Are you feeling rebellious, Alexa? Perhaps you feel you know better?"

His tone was mild but she sensed the anger in it, an anger deeper than any mere annoyance he'd ever shown her. She sat farther back in her chair. Her shoulders hunched.

"There's just so much to remember," she said.

Even without looking up she felt his gaze on her, his coal black eyes glaring from across the table. His anger had an almost acrid smell, a burning blast-wave of pressure. She wanted to cringe away, crawl under the table, prostate herself at his feet, beg his forgiveness...

The pressure vanished. She glanced up to see him taking a sip of his drink, looking off to the right at the chalkboard menu on the wall. A wave of dizziness swept over her. She grabbed onto her drink, sloshing some over her hand and onto the table.

"Be careful," he said.

"Yes, Constantine," she said.

He smiled at her. "Good girl. Now drink your beer."

A minor punishment now that he knew she didn't like it. Still she lifted the glass to her lips and sipped the tepid liquid.

"You're probably wondering why I had you meet me here in this pub," he said.

Should she admit to it? Would he take it as criticism? She didn't want to face his true wrath.

"No," she said. "I'll always meet you wherever you like."

He frowned. "Don't lie to me, Alexa, even if you think it's what I want to hear."

She winced. Would he punish now? Her hand trembled, sloshing more beer onto the table. She pulled her hand from the glass and held it on her lap, feeling the sticky liquid smear on her skirt.

"Relax," he said. "Now you know what I want to hear. I do not punish for learning, only for disobedience."

"Yes, Constantine," she said.

"We are here because I have some very important lessons for you," he said. "Drink up, Alexa."

She brought her hand back up and grabbed the glass to take another sip of beer.

"I have business to attend to. These In-Between have become too disruptive for us. We are now allowed to take action," he said.

Allowed.

Even Constantine answered to someone else.

It wasn't the first time Constantine had hinted at a greater authority in the vampire realm. He hadn't told her much beyond the fact that he was head of his clan and all in the clan deferred to him. He made the choice of who could be turned and more often than not would be the one doing the turning. Any who disobeyed would be punished.

Except for Bianca, who had managed to escape before Constantine could catch up with her.

"And that's happening near here?" she said.

He nodded, smiling. Alexa felt a rush of relief. She'd pleased him. He would not punish her when she pleased him.

"Sometimes one of the human cattle comes too close to the truth about us. When that happens, we must stop it." His smile widened. "That means stopping them." His smile faded. "But sometimes the In-Between hear of it before us and they act as body guards against us. That makes it a little more challenging."

Alexa heard the anger in his voice and tasted how his scent turned sour.

It made her want to crawl under the table again and it wasn't even aimed at her. How could any In-Between stand against him? She knew now from her own turning that the In-Between must have some of her ability to sense others' emotions. Sebastian had never told her as such but now she realized he must have felt it. How could any of them stand against Constantine then? She couldn't understand it.

"Is there someone like that near here?" she said.

"Yes, an old scholar who's been collecting obscure texts. We think he's got hold of one of our sacred books."

She sipped at her beer. "Sacred books?"

"We do have them," he said. "Writings from some of the oldest vampires. Some of it is drivel but some of it is quite prophetic. They were written by hand. We didn't have floppy disks back then."

Floppy disks, what were those? But she didn't want to ask. She didn't want to take the chance and make him angry again.

"How could he have gotten one of these books?" she said.

His lips thinned and she again smelled the sourness of his anger, rising in strength. Her shoulders hunched. Her hands tightened on the glass, holding it in front of her like a shield.

"An attack on one of our libraries in California," he said. "It burned to the ground. Some said the books went up in flames but I never believed it. I knew the In-Between were behind it and that they'd staged the fire to make off with our books. A few have started to turn up in different places. Now *they* have to pay attention."

She heard the emphasis on the word. Who were "they?" She didn't dare interrupt him to ask.

"There are rumors one of the books is here in England with this scholar. He's being guarded by In-Between, which lends credence to it. We will take care of any bodyguards and then deal with the scholar. I want him alive for questioning but the bodyguards can be killed."

A thrill ran through her at the mention of killing. Then she frowned. "We can kill them but we can't feed from them, right?"

"That's right. They're spoiled so we won't waste much time on them."

"Is the rest of the clan helping or is it just us?"

"The others will be there. I wanted to brief you alone. This will be your first battle, Alexa. It is a right of passage. You need to be prepared for it. Do you have any questions?"

She nodded. "The In-Between, how do we kill them if we can't feed? Can we even bite them?"

"Best not to," he said. "Even a little of their blood will make a vampire sick, especially you. You are still a child."

She bristled a little at his comment. She'd had her share of kills. How could he call her a child?

He laughed at her reaction. "Easy, Alexa. That spirit shows me you are already moving beyond the child phase. I encourage that, but remember I demand obedience. Something to keep in mind as you grow. As for the In-Between, while we can't bite, we can still claw them." He smiled. "None of them are immune to the ripped out throat."

"Or snapped neck?" she said.

He nodded. "Or snapped neck."

She smiled. "When do we go?"

Constantine insisted they finish their beers before they left. She resigned herself to swallowing the tepid liquid and was a little dismayed when Constantine signaled to the waitress. He was going to order another round, she thought. Would he let her choose a different drink, something she used to like at least? But instead of ordering another round, he took hold of the waitress's wrist.

"Come," he said and stood up. Alexa scrambled to follow as he headed toward the back of the bar. The waitress kept in step, a blank expression on her face. As they walked through the crowd, Alexa noticed how none of the patrons or bar staff looked their way. Constantine was a master at clouding minds.

She so wanted to learn to do that.

They slipped through the kitchen unseen and into the back alley behind the bar. A single bare bulb illuminated the alley, weak light barely penetrating more than a few feet beyond the doorway. Two grimy blue dumpsters sat in the shadows to the right. The odor of rotting vegetables and decaying meat drifted in the air. Uneven asphalt led to the left, toward the street and the hum of passing traffic. The dull red brick walls rose several stories above them, fading into darkness beyond the reach of that single light bulb.

Constantine dragged the waitress into the shadows.

"Remember," he said to Alexa. "When doing a general feeding it's best not to take all the blood. If they haven't seen you at all, you can even let them live. That way you can keep feeding off them. They'll carry your scent and be marked as yours to other vampires. It's always good to have a stable supply. But if they've seen you for any length of time, it's best to make the kill. Leave enough blood to make some mess and drink the rest." He smiled. "Best not to upset the cattle too much."

He lifted his hand to the waitress's neck and slashed. She gasped as the flesh of her neck parted. For a moment, the wound gaped clean then the blood began to flow, running down her neck, staining the front of her white uniform. She staggered. Constantine tightened his grip, holding her upright. He nodded to Alexa.

"Let's have a snack."

He bent to drink first as was his due. When he finished, he held the waitress out to Alexa, who tipped her head to drink.

Blood flooded her mouth. As always the taste made her euphoric. She couldn't believe she'd enjoyed anything so much, not any food or drink or sex. She could feel the woman's life flowing through the blood, filling her with power and energy. Her whole body tingled with pleasure. She fastened her mouth to the wound to suck more into her mouth. The warmth smeared her cheeks and spilled onto her shirt.

She would have drank and drank but she felt Constantine's hand on her shoulder. After a moment, his fingers dug in, signaling that she was finished. With reluctance, she lifted her head away. Blood still pumped from the woman's throat. Such a waste. Alexa licked her lips.

Constantine dropped the body to the ground then he stooped to tear the clothing. He lifted her skirt and left her exposed. Then he stood up.

"There, they'll think it was just a sex attack," he said. "That's why you don't drink it all. Leave enough for them to find and make sure it's a sufficient amount. Can't make the cattle suspicious." He reached out, wrapping his fingers in her hair and turning her head to face him. "Do you understand, Alexa?"

His fingers tightened on her hair, informing her this was an important lesson to remember.

"Yes, Constantine," she said.

"Good girl." He released her. "Let's go. Wipe your face."

She grabbed the rag that had been tucked into the waitress's belt and followed him into the night.

The house looked like some large estate out of an old British mini-series: two stories high, wider than two regular houses combined, with turrets on either side, but even from the road Alexa could tell it had seen better days. Flaking paint on old brick and crumbling concrete around the foundation indicated it had been years since there had been any major upkeep. The lawn, while cut, was patchy with yellowish spots. A neglected garden crossed the front of the house, empty but for some straggly weeds.

She breathed in the night air, scenting the presence of several people. She looked over at Constantine. He stood closer to the main gate, flanked by his two main confidantes, Bruno and Helena. They all held their heads together but didn't seem to speak, at least she wasn't able to make out their lips moving. Were they even talking at all? Were they able to communicate telepathically? She itched to know but they wouldn't tell her. Although Constantine treated her mostly with respect, the others still treated her like a child.

It made her want to rip their throats out.

Light burst out from the side of the house. Alexa ducked back behind the stone wall she hid behind. Seeing the three scurry for cover almost made her smile.

An engine roared as the light began to move closer. A car, someone driving away from the house. Would Constantine signal them to stop it? She tensed her muscles, ready to jump.

No signal came. The car slowed at the gate, waiting for it swing open, then it drove through. It made a right signal and turned, speeding away. She watched it a moment and then looked back just in time to see Constantine's wave. She raced after the others as they poured through the open gate.

The vampires fanned out across the lawn, staying low to the ground as they ran. Alexa followed their examples, running in an almost crablike manner. As they approached the house, they slowed at an unspoken command. Alexa matched the others around her. She didn't feel it but could tell the others felt something by the way they jerked their heads.

She stood with Vera, another vampire woman, just under a second story window. They flanked either side. Vera stared at the window as if expecting something to happen. Alexa followed her example, glancing at her several times to make sure Vera wasn't doing anything else. After a moment, she heard a large pop. The lights went out. Alexa saw Vera smile.

Vera leapt for the window. She landed on the half-inch wide ledge. Her right arm swung and she slammed it into the glass. The window shattered, collapsing into the room as Vera jumped through. Alexa crouched and jumped, sailing through the shattered remains.

Throughout the house, she heard echoes of shattering glass, followed by yells and shouts. In the darkness, she dodged the desk and armchair, following Vera through the door. The interior hallway was black but Alexa had no trouble seeing. She didn't even really need her glasses anymore, she just liked the way they looked on her nose.

Vera headed right. Alexa went left. A figure stepped out of a doorway a few feet down. She saw a weapon clutched in its hand. Alexa snarled and slashed. The figure tried to duck but she caught him in the face. He slammed against the wall. The weapon, some kind of gun, skidded down the hall. The man lunged after it.

Alexa leapt onto his back. The urge to plunge her teeth into his neck almost overwhelmed her. In fact, she found herself yanking the collar of his shirt back, preparing to bite when she remembered. In-Between. Poison! Instead, she grabbed the sides of his head. His fingers reached the gun. Her grip tightened and she wrenched to the left. A satisfying snap sounded. The body beneath her legs shuddered and flopped.

Her first kill in battle! Excitement surged through her. Constantine would be proud. She had to show him. She pressed her foot against the neck and yanked. Cartilage tore but the head stayed attached. Dammit! She used her nails to slice around the neck then wrenched again. One last effort and the head popped off. She stumbled backward. Her fingers wrapped in the hair and she carried her prize off.

The scent of blood and battle led her deeper into the house. She ran, trailing blood from the head behind her. The tiled hallway ended at a large marble foyer at the front of the house. She crouched in the doorway, watching. Black clothed men battled the vampires. They used small, machete-like swords, hacking and slicing at the vampires that darted close, slashing with claws. Above them, she noticed a few silent figures creeping along the balcony that faced down on the foyer. They looked like they were carrying a weapon similar to her friend here. Four of them, if she could see correctly and none of the vampires fighting below had seen them.

None but her.

She wouldn't be able to make it through the fighters to the stairway so she retreated back down the hall. Old houses like this had secondary stairs, usually through the kitchen. She remembered that from several of the frat parties she'd been to at college. Odd to have those memories in this context. The last party she'd been to had been the night, yes, it was the night Sebastian had been attacked. She'd been waiting to talk to him then, maybe see if with enough alcohol, he would summon the courage to ask her out.

It seemed like centuries ago.

She ran down the hall and found the kitchen. Just like she thought, a small stairway led up to the second floor. Even with her short legs, she sped up the stairs two at a time. A hallway stretched out before her, parallel to the one below. She raced forward, building up speed. The hallway curved, then the right wall dropped away. A railing extended onward. The balcony!

She bared her teeth and leapt forward, swinging the head. Her charge overwhelmed the first two. They'd been leaning over the railing, aiming their weapons. She knocked them flying. They soared over the railing, dropping to the floor below.

The final two noticed and turned to meet her but it was too late. She had momentum now. She slammed into the third one. His weapon flew from his hand. A slash with her left hand opened his throat. He managed a gurgle before he fell to his knees.

The fourth brought his weapon up and fired. She felt a bullet hit her left shoulder. Pain blossomed, making her hiss. She grabbed the third man, and tossed him forward. Bullets sprayed the wall and ceiling as the fourth man tried to dodge. Even as he brought the gun back toward her, Alexa was moving. She swung the head. The gun went flying. Snarling, she leapt on the man and tore his throat out with her teeth.

It took all her self control to spit out the blood but she did it and wiped her mouth on her arm. The pain in her shoulder burned. Should a bullet hurt that much?

She staggered to the stairs and headed down them. Below her, she saw the vampires mopping up. Two of the In-Between knelt by the front door. Two vampires stood behind them, holding their arms back and up, forcing them forward. The other men lay unmoving.

Constantine stepped out of a room beside the front door. His hands clenched into fists. Even at a distance in the dark, Alexa could see the fury on his face. The stench of it billowed across the room. It seemed to intensify the pain in her shoulder. Alexa reached the floor and sagged against the banister.

Constantine stormed across the foyer to the two men. "Where is it?" he said.

Neither men spoke. Constantine grabbed the first one by the throat, lifting him up. The man choked and struggled but the vampire behind him held his arms fast.

"Was it in that car that left?" Constantine said. "How did you know we'd be coming?"

The man's mouth open and closed but no words came out. Constantine tightened his grip. His claws pierced the man's skin. Blood dripped down and spread in a black stain on the white marble floor.

"Where is it?" Constantine roared.

"Gone." The second man's voice was a bare whisper but everyone froze at the word.

Constantine growled. His fist clenched. Nails dug into the first man's throat. He bucked and wrenched, then sagged in death. Constantine dropped him.

"Where?" he said to the second man.

The man shook his head. "Don't know. We were just told to move it."

"When? How?"

More head shaking. "Don't know. You'd been set up, mate."

"What do you mean set up?"

The man barked out a laugh. "Who else knows your kind wants that book? You think you're the first clan to look for it?" His laugh sounded choked, then ceased to be a laugh when Constantine snarled. He slashed the man across the face. Blood splashed against the door and the body shuddered. The vampire holding his arms let go. The body flopped to the floor.

"Out," Constantine said.

As one, the vampires started moving toward the door. Alexa tried to follow, dragging her head with her, the head from her first kill. But her shoulder burned, pain streak across her chest and down her body. She staggered, then righted herself, then staggered again. She bumped into a body on the floor. The stumble made her fall to her knees. She tried to push up but found she couldn't rise.

Vera walked past her and then looked back. "Come on, kid, let's go."

"I..." Even talking was hard now. The pain radiated up into her skull.

Vera peered closer. "What's that on your shoulder?"

"Bullet," Alexa managed.

Her eyes felt heavy. She'd close them just for a moment and then she'd follow. She heard Vera's voice yelling for Constantine and something about a silver bullet, then the soothing darkness claimed her.

Part One: Remembrance

CHAPTER ONE

Even with the darkest sunglasses, long sleeves, and a ball cap with the brim covering his face, the headache still started as soon as Sebastian stepped out into the sun. Even with the special drug Octenphotohistra, developed by one of the In-Between scientists, his sensitivity still bordered on painful.

After a year, he was almost used to the agony and expected it as soon as he stepped outside when it wasn't night. A year since he'd been a normal college student, heading into the finish of his third year, and the biggest challenge was to gather the courage to ask out the woman he loved on a date. A year since a walk in the trees just off campus after a party had left him trapped between human and vampire, one of the In-Between, stuck with the sun sensitivity and some of the other heightened senses of vampires but also with the desire for blood.

It meant he couldn't go back, couldn't be that normal college student ever again. And it had also led to the death of his best friend at the hands of the woman he loved, a woman turned into a vampire as revenge and threat against Sebastian.

It still hurt to think about that so he didn't do it very often. Instead he focused on now, on learning how to survive as an In-Between. On how to deal with who he was now, and all the continuing challenges.

Like surviving during sunlight hours.

Having an overcast day like today was almost a blessing. He didn't want to rip his head off within the first five minutes.

Instead he wanted to rip off Nigel's head.

"Hurry up, Sebastian, we've only got a couple of hours for the reconnaissance."

The man's nasal twang seemed especially exasperated. Beside Sebastian's height, Nigel's short frame looked even shorter, as if he'd been squished. Limp brown hair hung in a shaggy cut around his narrow head. Standing almost six inches above him, Sebastian could see how Nigel styled it to cover several balding spots. His thin mouth was forever in a perpetual frown, narrow lips thinned even more as they pressed together. He had watery grey eyes, a nose too big for his face (hence the nasal twang) and his shoulders hunched as if he was always carrying a backpack.

From his almost constant glares, Sebastian knew Nigel didn't like him either. So much for the brotherhood and camaraderie among the In-Between that he'd expected.

Funny how they seemed just like regular people, with all the strengths and foibles.

Sebastian paused to zip up his hoodie and tuck it around the back of his neck. Even with the cloudy sky, he didn't like to take chances that the sun might decide to peak out at him. Nigel's sigh made him just a little slower, then he stuck his hands in his pockets.

"Okay, let's go."

They headed down the cobblestone street. This late in the afternoon the street was deserted. A light breeze blew toward them, carrying the scent of the sea. Sebastian had been smelling it the whole time they'd been in Calais. It almost made him seasick.

Nigel turned and led him down a narrow side street. They passed a park on the left. From here Sebastian could hear the rustle of the grass as people walked along. Children shouted in the distance.

It took another ten minutes before they found a suitable car. The owner, a short plump young woman with a mass of blond curls piled on top of her head, was just locking the driver's side door. She had her purse slung over her shoulder and carried an empty nylon bag, a sure sign she was heading out to buy groceries.

Sebastian and Nigel stood across the street under an unlit street lamp. Nigel waited until she'd finished locking the car. She hitched her purse up over her shoulder and was about to stick the keys inside it.

"Now," he said to Sebastian.

"Shouldn't we wait for someone else?" Sebastian said. He had a feeling the woman was buying food for her family.

"You see anybody else? Do it, dammit, or I will."

Sebastian had seen Nigel at work. He was crude and forceful, leaving both physical and mental pain behind. No, Sebastian couldn't let him do it.

"Fine." Sebastian stuck his hands in his pockets and crossed the narrow street.

Unfortunately, the woman had put her keys in her purse and had started moving around the front of the car. She was heading for the bakery just down the block, he thought. He had to get to her before she made it.

She managed one foot up onto the sidewalk before he got close enough to call to her.

"Pardon, mademoiselle," he said.

He spoke quietly, forcing her to focus more attention to hear him. She turned toward him, her eyebrows rising in curiosity. Her left hand clutched her purse strap to her side.

"Ne vous parler anglais?"

"Oui, yes," she said. She held up her hand with her fingers an inch apart. "Little."

"Ah bon, good," he said. He was starting to suspect it didn't matter but it certainly made things easier for him. "I want you to give me your car."

He tilted his head down, staring right into her eyes. For a moment they widened in surprise at his outrageous request then they started to defocus. He waited another moment before reaching out to touch her hand holding onto the strap of her purse. The fingers opened and her hand flopped to her side.

"The car will be waiting here for you tomorrow," he said. "If that is all right."

"Oui, yes, of course." Her voice had a distant sound to it, an almost dreamy, lilting quality.

He knew Nigel would be annoyed that he promised to return the car but he didn't feel right just taking it and leaving it somewhere. The least they could do was return it. He would just make sure they wiped all the surfaces down.

"You won't need to remember me," he said. He reached into her purse. On the side closest to her, he felt an interior pocket. Lumpy. Yes, there were the keys.

He pulled them out. "Are these just the car keys?"

"Non," she said. "My house keys and the shed in the back."

"Which ones?" he said. Her hand lifted, wavering. He held the keys out to her. She picked two keys. He unfastened them from the key ring and slipped them back into the inside pocket of her purse.

"You decided to take those keys off your key ring," he said. "It's dangerous to carry your house keys on your car key ring. You were going to get a new key ring today for your house keys."

"Yes," she said. "A new key ring."

"Go do your shopping," he said. "Take your time. Do not come back for at least two hours."

"Oui, yes." She turned away from him. Her foot slipped off the step onto the sidewalk. He flinched and just stopped himself from reaching for her. Any further contact could break his Influence on her or Bind her to him. He didn't want to deal with either possibility.

She stepped up again and this time continued on down the sidewalk. He waited until she had reached the door to the bakery and pulled it open, stepping inside without a further glance in his direction. He turned to find Nigel standing at the driver's door.

He held out his hand. "I'll drive. I know the way."

Better to not argue. He handed over the keys.

They headed east out of the city. Sebastian glanced around Nigel, but with the dullness of the sky could barely see the sea on the left. So much for the white cliffs of Dover. Maybe he'd come out one clear evening and see if he could see them.

A Remembrance of Flesh

The drive took almost two hours, cutting it close as far as Sebastian was concerned, but the timing hadn't been his decision. Morgan called the shots in their tiny cell. With half the group in Paris and not expected until late tonight, they needed the target scouted as soon as possible.

Nigel pulled onto a side road. Cracked, older pavement made for a bumpy ride but they only drove far enough to not be seen from the main road. Nigel pulled over to the side and shut off the car.

"Now follow me and keep your head down. Chances are they'll be asleep but they might have sentries watching. They don't like sunlight but some of them have a higher tolerance, especially in weather like this."

He gave Sebastian a suspicious look and opened the driver's side door, slipping outside. Sebastian's lips thinned. He had had quite enough of Nigel's attitude. Steady. He got out of the car. They were two hours outside Calais. He had no doubt that Nigel would have no trouble stranding him out here.

And outside a farm house full of vampires wasn't the place he wanted to be abandoned.

They crossed the road and headed into the small field. Sebastian breathed in the scent of wild grass and clover, sweet and clean. Some withering stocks of something, wheat maybe, still grew in the ground but the field had been left to grow wild. He'd heard that some farmers did that with their fields, rotating through them to give the ground a chance to rest between seasons, but this field had the feel of long abandonment. The grass reached their knees as they trudged through. At least there were the barest indications of old rows.

They walked for almost ten minutes before Sebastian caught a glimpse of something in the distance. He resisted the urge to do a close up focus. It would just intensify his headache. He already felt it throbbing in his temples and stretching down his neck, tensing his shoulders. Much more and he'd have a hard time getting back to the car.

Like the others, Nigel didn't seem to have as much of a problem with the sunlight as Sebastian. They all took the Octenphotohistra in smaller doses which reduced the effect of sunlight to nil. Naturally, it didn't work as well on him, even at the higher dosage. But without it, he could barely function at all in the sunlight.

He couldn't tell them that. He couldn't let them know.

He didn't want to give them another reason to be suspicious of him.

Another few minutes of trudging and the suggestion of something on the horizon gelled into an old, white brick farmhouse. Wood shutters covered the windows, the brown paint long since faded from sun and weather. A crumbling chimney rose from the back end of the roof, probably where the kitchen was, Sebastian thought. It look cozy and quaint, someone's home, probably the farmer who should be tilling these fields. But the house held the same abandoned air to it, even from this distance.

Nigel made a chopping hand signal and they slowed to a stop, crouching down among the wild grass. Sebastian breathed in the scent of the grass and earth. From the rich scent, he could tell that it had rained here within the last few days. It would probably rain again soon from the look of the sky.

As long as the rain held off for a few days. Let it wait until then. This would be a lot easier without the rain.

"Focus on the house," Nigel said. "Let's see if we can figure out how many there are."

Sebastian rested one hand on the ground, feeling hard packed earth beneath loose soil. The pain in his temples throbbed as he stared at the house. With each eye blink, he had a strong sense of it. The white brick had a layer of dirt that dulled the paint. The wood shutters hung at slight angles, resting against each other on rusting hinges, the paint long weathered from the slightly bowing slates. But it didn't matter that the slates didn't sit quite tight enough together anymore, Sebastian found. Inside the house, someone had tacked up blankets and covers over the windows, blocking out any stray sunlight that might shine through on a sunny day.

Inside the house, he caught brief glimpses. Bare furnishings in the rooms. Peeling paint. Empty cupboards in the kitchen, standing open. Missing appliances. Just off the kitchen, a smaller door. This one was freshly painted and fit snug in its frame. It locked from the inside and led downward. A basement? Not the same kind he was used to at home in the States, this was more of a cold storage area. But now the dim, dark, moist area deep in the ground kept something other than vegetables away from the harsh light.

How many? That was what they were here to find out.

The headache now pounded at his temples, like someone knocking on the inside of his skull. Concentrate on the house, on the cold storage area. Focus.

He pushed the pain to the back of his mind where it throbbed its constant reminder. He would pay for this effort; just let him pay for it later, not now.

He felt the cold storage area like a cool, dark place inside his mind. Irregularly shaped, the walls sloped inward toward the low ceiling. They'd dug more of it out, he realized, trying to make the space bigger, to accommodate more of them. How many more? How many of them? He felt the suggestion of them in there, a coldness deeper in his mind than any temperature. Each one felt a little different. If he concentrated enough, he might be able to tell... yes, there, one, two... He started counting up the slight variations all the way up to six. Was that right? Yes, he almost pulled away but another flutter caught his attention, something behind the other six. He started counting again. Seven, eight, and onward to thirteen. Thirteen, a baker's dozen. That seemed to be all there were.

Any others in the house? He pulled his attention from the cold storage area and tried to cast it around the interior of the house but his focus dissipated. The pain bloomed in his head, demanding attention. His muscles trembled. He sagged on the ground, now pressing both hands on the dirt, supporting himself. He felt sweat drip down the sides of his face. His heart thudded in his chest.

Enough.

"Thirteen in a cold storage area off the kitchen," he said.

Nigel's frown filled his vision when he opened his eyes.

"That's not what I got," Nigel said. "I only got six."

"I got six at first," Sebastian said. "Then I felt something behind that, a kind of flutter. Then I found the others."

"A flutter," Nigel said. "Are you sure you aren't aflutter?"

Annoyance made Sebastian thin his lips. "I found thirteen. Why don't you recheck? Morgan wanted us to be thorough."

Invoking Morgan's name made Nigel flare his nostrils. Morgan didn't care for minor squabbles, was only interested in results and would lambast them both if he thought they hadn't done a proper job. It didn't matter who was at fault, they would both be reprimanded.

"I'll check again," Nigel said. He turned more than necessary, making sure his back was to Sebastian.

Sebastian stuck out his tongue.

He could feel Nigel's attention shift to the house, almost feel Nigel's skin cool as his energy went into his concentration. Did Sebastian get that cold? He didn't think he did but he couldn't tell. No one had ever mentioned it, not even Jessica.

He pushed the thought of her away. He hadn't seen her for almost six weeks, since Morgan had sent her with the others to rendezvous with the group from the UK. He hadn't wanted her to go, had even come close to saying something but he knew it would just cause tension and problems for her. Fraternization was discouraged but tolerated as long as people were discreet. He knew Jessica wouldn't appreciate him jeopardizing her position.

Finally Nigel shifted. Sebastian felt the man's temperature rise even before he opened his eyes and turned around.

"I only got six," Nigel said. "That's two readings. We'll go with that."

"But..."

"Look." Nigel held up a hand to stop him. "I know you're supposed to be some super In-Between or something but you've only had it for a year. I've been In-Between for over seven. I know the condition more than you. You felt an echo, that's all. You aren't the first. When you get more experience, you'll be able to read better. Until then, remember that every mission you go on is still training for you."

He stood up, brushing dirt from his pants. "Let's get back to the car."

"Wait a minute." Sebastian scrambled to his feet and hurried to catch up. Nigel strode down the overgrown row, moving farther away from the house.

"Shouldn't we do a physical check of the outside of the house?" Sebastian said.

"Why? We're to do reconnaissance on the vampires not look into housing design."

"They might have fortified the structure, made it harder to get into."

"You know, we have done this before." Nigel's voice dripped sarcasm.

The urge to rip off his head rose up again in Sebastian but now Nigel was too far ahead. He'd never get a good grip on that weasley little head.

They reached the narrow road. Still deserted in either direction. Nigel crossed the street, heading again for the driver's side. Sebastian sighed. He could volunteer to go back and check out the house physically himself but he didn't trust that Nigel wouldn't drive away without him.

"Are you coming?" Nigel called through the open window.

Sebastian hurried across to the passenger's seat. Even before he got the seat belt on, Nigel hit the gas, sending the car jolting ahead. Sebastian banged his shoulder against the doorframe.

"Ow, hey."

"Oh sorry," Nigel said. "I thought you were settled."

He had the hint of a smirk on his narrow face.

Sebastian could reach his head now, yank it right off his neck, off his shoulders and toss it out the open window.

And he might have even done it if he'd been the one driving.

They ditched the car back near the place where they found it. Sebastian insisted it be some place easy for the woman to find it again. He didn't like causing her any more anguish than necessary. Nigel merely shook his head.

The sky darkened as they made their way back to the old three story walkup. Sebastian welcomed the night, removing his cap and sunglasses, stuffing them into the pockets of his hoodie. With the dark came an influx of energy. He felt it in his muscles and in the heightening of his senses. Smells, already sharp, became even sharper. Sounds became crisp and focused. He heard a woman calling in French to her son three blocks away. The hum of early evening traffic on the main streets. The clink of glasses inside the café at the corner. And in the background of it all, like an ever present hum, the steady whooshing flow of the ocean, clawing at the beach as if to overtake it.

As they reached the old building, Sebastian pushed his senses to the maximum, trolling for any sign of vampires. A couple turned onto the street a block down, walking arm in arm along the sidewalk. Sebastian took a deep breath, smelling the spicy fragrance of the woman's cologne and the man's musky sweat. Layered beneath, he smelled the warm humanness of their skin and the tang of their blood.

Not vampire. Definitely.

Nigel took one final scout around and nodded to Sebastian. They crossed the street, heading for the black, peeling door beside the bakery. Beyond the door, narrow stairs led up. Sebastian closed the door behind him, plunging the stairs into blackness. The bulb hanging from the ceiling had burned out years ago, they'd told him, and no one had replaced it. But even pitch black didn't matter to the In-Between. Sebastian had to wait only a moment for his eyes to adjust. Then he followed Nigel up the stairs.

What a difference these stairs were from the stairwell in his old dorm an ocean away.

Where had that thought come from? He hadn't thought about the dorm or the college in months. That was a different time, a different life. He wasn't that person anymore. Sure he still looked the same, still the same tall, black-haired young man but now he moved with a sliding grace, like the other In-Between. He'd gained more than just a scar on the side of his neck from the attack by the vampire Bianca, but he'd lost so much more. So much, that even comparing these stairs to the ones at school brought him too close to memories best left buried. Too close to Charlie, now dead for over a year. Too close to Alexa, now lost for over a year.

No, not lost, admit it. She was the vampire who killed Charlie after all.

His head bowed.

Stop it, just stop it.

He forced his churning emotions down as he reached the top of the stairs. A multitude of voices attracted his attention, more voices than he expected. He pushed through into the main room.

A group of fifteen In-Between crammed into the main room, sitting on the sagging couches, perched on the mismatched chairs. A few even lounged on cushions on the floor. Across the large room that took up half of this floor, he spotted Jessica leaning against the wall, her arms folded over her chest, her ever present dark ponytail draped over her shoulder. She looked exactly the same as when he'd first seen her in the college library over a year ago, down to the same posture and tilt of her head. She was smiling at something one of the men sitting on the floor said, then her head lifted and she spotted him. The smile didn't waver but she lifted her chin higher in greeting.

He started to head across the room to her when he noticed Nigel talking to Morgan. Morgan was nodding, then as Nigel finished, held up his hands for silence. The talking in the room dropped off. Sebastian found himself in the center of the room. He stepped back to stand beside the door and gave Jessica a tiny shrug. Her chin ducked in a nod of understanding.

"First folks, I want to say welcome back to our returned brothers and sisters. We're glad you're back safely. I'm reviewing their reports and will share it with the rest of you once all the analysis is done. I wish I could say we have time to relax but we've learned of a nest a few hours away. We know the vampires are trying to consolidate their numbers here in Europe. It used to be we could count on the clans fighting to help us with our goals but they seem to be more cooperative these days. We haven't figured out why but we're in touch with other cells."

Morgan nodded at Nigel. "While you lot were away, we sent Nigel to recon the nest. He's come back with a report."

Nigel nodded a thanks to Morgan and took a step farther into the room. He stood at stiff, hands behind his back, legs shoulder width apart as if he was on some kind of parade rest, Sebastian thought. He noticed that Morgan hadn't mentioned him at all, probably because Nigel hadn't bothered to tell him.

"The location is a two hour drive straight east of here," Nigel said. "It's a white brick farmhouse, abandoned, surrounded by open fields. It's a short distance off the main road but isn't easily seen from there. A multi-angle approach would be best to block any exit from the farm house. Surveillance indicated six targets inside."

Sebastian pushed away from the wall.

"No," he said. "There were thirteen."

The multitude of faces turned to look at him. Nigel scowled. "You felt echoes. There were only six." He turned back to face the group. "I confirmed it twice. Six. Sebastian is still learning. Obviously he doesn't have the experience to fully read properly. Why he..."

"That's enough," Morgan said.

"It was thirteen," Sebastian repeated.

"I said enough," Morgan said. His voice cut through the quiet murmurs that had started. Silence filled the room. "Nigel is an experienced recon man, we'll go with his reading and we'll prepare for more just in case. I want to hit them just after dawn so that means a three am departure. Everyone get some rest. We'll reconvene at three to head out."

Voices filled the area as Morgan finished and turned away. Sebastian ignored Nigel's smirk as he crossed the room to Jessica. She raised an eyebrow in bemusement.

"You just can't let things go, can you?" she said.

He opened his mouth then closed it as someone brushed past him. "Not here."

She pushed away from the wall and slipped her hand around his arm. "Then let's go for a walk. We were stuck in that van for ages. I want some air."

She dragged him back down the stairs and into the night.

Cool air filled his nostrils with the tang of salt water. He could almost feel the mist of it on his skin. He allowed Jessica to steer him away from the building, aiming in a wandering path toward the ocean. Almost automatically she took a route that avoided people, avoided the temptation of the scent of their blood. She was so much better at that than he was but she had five years more experience than him.

After several blocks, she slowed her pace to a leisurely walk. "So. About Nigel," she said. "Tell me what happened there."

"Nothing happened there," he said. "Except that he's an ass."

"That he is," she said. "But he's a well respected ass because he's a good recon man, can sniff out vampires a mile or more away. You won't get anywhere contradicting him."

"Even when he's wrong?" he said. "And he is. There were thirteen vampires in that house."

"Come on, Sebastian, that's a crazy number," she said. "The most we've seen together is ten. Most clans level off at seven or eight."

"I don't claim to understand it," he said. "But there were thirteen in that house. I think Nigel sensed it too, after I brought it to his attention. He just doesn't want to admit I'm right."

"Why would he when you're contradicting him in front of everyone? That's not how you do this."

"Sorry I'm not up on the social niceties," he said. "I thought we were In-Between and trying to stop the vampires."

"You've certainly gotten testy," she said. "You weren't like this when I met you."

"Seeing your best friend ripped apart by the woman you love does that to you," he said.

She didn't say anything.

Dammit, he thought, he never should have said that. Why couldn't he learn when to shut up?

They walked on for another moment then her hand tightened on his arm, pulling him to a stop. She turned to face him. The soft light from the street lamp half a block away made the caramel highlights glow in her hair. Her expression was serious.

"Sebastian, I know this has been a hard year for you. I know losing both Charlie and Alexa made it even harder but you have to realize we all went through the same thing. We all lost our old lives and had to build new ones. I know it's hard only being able to deal with In-Between and not being able to talk to other people because the smell of their blood drives you crazy. And believe me, I know Nigel is a jerk but you could try a little harder to get along."

His shoulders sagged. She was right and he knew it. It was just so exasperating with the others. Even after a year he seemed more susceptible to the sun, had more problems around regular people, and still got swayed too much by the stronger vampires.

"I'm sorry," he said.

She nodded. A small smile played at the corners of her lips. "Mind you, I'd pay to see you punch Nigel in the head."

"I don't really want to hurt my hand like that."

"I can lend you my brass knuckles. Or a baseball bat."

"A bat is kind of outside the punching idea."

"You don't have to be so literal," she said. "What happened to the spirit of the thing?"

She laced her arm back through his and they started walking again.

"I think a golf club would be better," he said.

"Hmm, you'll have to wait until we head over to Ireland, then you can hit him on a golf course and no one will bat an eye."

"That is evil," he said.

"Why? You don't think he deserves it?" she said.

"Now I didn't say that."

She smiled and changed their direction, leading them down to the sea.

CHAPTER TWO

The alarm went off, the buzzer shrieking in the night.

Sebastian buried his head deeper in the blanket. It was Friday, he didn't have a class until eleven, he didn't have to be up so early. He pulled his arm from beneath the blanket and slapped around at the night stand. His hand felt nothing, just air. He continued waving. Someone grabbed his wrist. A woman's voice spoke in his ear.

"Sebastian, wake up. It's time to get ready for the raid."

His eyes snapped open. He bolted upright. Jessica released his arm and stepped back.

"I'll meet you out back," she said.

He nodded, not willing to speak. Speaking would shatter the remaining threads of his dream, a dream where he was still at college. Charlie was still alive and Alexa wasn't a vampire. A dream where his worst nightmare was trying to find a shirt without a food stain on it and surviving the statistics class.

Now those nightmares were his dearest dreams.

The images faded, the last one to go of Charlie and Alexa sitting around the dorm room, her sitting with legs crossed on the office chair and Charlie sprawled on the bed. How Sebastian wished he'd realized those were the best days of his life, but they were just ordinary. Nothing special.

Now they were gone.

He dressed and was out back within five minutes and still he managed to be one of the stragglers. Morgan was already dividing people up into their teams. They would drive in convoy to the house, attack and split up, rendezvousing three days from now at the agreed upon spot. Of course only the select few in each team knew the location, the easier to hide it from the vampires and their psychic abilities.

Sebastian scanned the crowd and spotted Jessica over to the right, standing with a group by a large black SUV. She lifted her head. He started toward her.

"Sebastian, you're with Fredrick's team." Morgan's voice halted his progress.

Sebastian turned. "Ah, what? I thought I could go with Arlene's team."

"They have enough," Morgan said. "Go with Fredrick."

Sebastian turned back toward Jessica. Her lips pressed together. She gave a little shrug.

"Come on, Sebastian, let's get a move on." Fredrick's baritone voice called to him.

He turned to follow Fredrick to an old brown station wagon.

<hr>

The station wagon had barely any shocks and struggled to go over seventy kilometers an hour. As the other cars sped away, Sebastian found himself bumping along in the soon to be last place.

At least Nigel wasn't in the same car.

They reached the house half an hour after everyone else. Fredrick parked the car farther along the side street, coming to rest under a small grove of trees. The four of them piled out. Fredrick gave shotguns to two of them. He took a crossbow and handed a machete to Sebastian.

"No shotgun?" Sebastian said.

"Your aim isn't good enough," Fredrick said. "We don't have the silver to waste. Now let's go."

Great, Sebastian thought, he wasn't even allowed to handle a weapon that could spray silver shot at a vampire. How much aiming ability did that take?

He trudged after them.

The dark still clung to the land but the dawn had already made inroads. A flush of color lightened the sky in the east. As he watched it, Sebastian realized he'd left his sunglasses back at the safe house. Dammit! He'd have a pounding headache by the time they got back, especially in that station wagon. Maybe he could beg a ride back with Jessica's group. The touch of her fingers on his temples always had a way of lessening the pain.

He pushed that thought away. Now he had to focus on the raid. He still thought they didn't have enough people for a raid of this sort. No matter how many times Nigel insisted, Sebastian knew there were thirteen vampires in that house. It wasn't any damn echo.

A breeze rustled the wild grass around him. For a moment he had an urge to slash at it with the machete as though he was in a jungle movie. If only the creature at the end of this path was a lion. But that was the real fantasy.

Ahead, Fredrick held up his hand, then pointed left. They began circling, still moving forward. Now Sebastian could see the house in the distance. The white brick seemed brighter in the fading darkness. He wondered if it shone in the middle of the night.

Around him, he could feel the presence of the other In-Between circling the house. If he concentrated enough, he might be able to pick out Jessica. He'd gotten better over time distinguishing their individual energy. It still unnerved him that he couldn't smell any of them, but at least he could sense their energy. He'd tried mentioning it to Morgan once. The man gave him a look like he was crazy. Sebastian didn't mention it again. He sensed that most of them already thought he was too far gone, too close to the edge of being a vampire, to be trusted. He didn't want to give them any other reasons to mistrust him. And since it had only started a month or so ago, he hadn't had a chance to talk to Jessica about it, to find out if anyone else had the same experience.

But for now, it allowed him the comfort of feeling the others surrounding the house. He could tell the four groups were at the four points of the house. As Fredrick held up a hand to signal a stop, Sebastian clenched his machete. He felt the other groups in place, poised and ready.

Dawn now definitely brightened the sky. The darkness had lost this match, retreating against the coming daylight. Streaks of yellow and orange blazed against the few clouds. The horizon glowed in the distance. A morning bird burst into song, the notes rising in the air.

The signal.

Fredrick's hand snapped up. They raced forward in a crouch, the four them spreading out in a line. From the other raids, Sebastian remembered, shotguns first, then crossbows, with machetes bringing up the rear. As they reached the rear door, he hung back.

The first man to reach the door crouched at the lock, the second man covering him. The door flew open. They ran inside.

Sebastian heard the crash of breaking glass, the slam of other doors opening, the thud of steps as the other groups flooded the house. He found himself in a ruined kitchen, worse than even his initial read from yesterday. Dirt and grime streaked the walls. Half the cupboard doors were missing, the rest hung open, warped with age. Darkness filled the room, not even the first rays of dawn peaked around the edges of the coverings on the windows.

His group headed forward. Sebastian sensed the door to the basement just to the left, but it felt strangely empty. He was about to speak when a snarl caught his attention.

Then all hell broke lose.

Vampires flooded the house. Several flew down the stairs from the second floor, crashing into the team that had entered through the front. Before they could react, half of that In-Between group died, throats ripped out. Sebastian heard the screams before the gurgle of death ended them.

Then he didn't have time to pay attention to the others.

A door on the right side of the kitchen slammed open. Two vampires jumped up, snarling. The men with the shotguns blasted at them, spraying silver buckshot. They caught the vampires full in the torso. Sebastian watched red bloom on the vampires's bodies. They howled, shaking their heads in anger and pain then continued moving forward. The men with the shotguns stepped back to reload and Fredrick raised his crossbow. As he let fly, one of the vampires leapt aside. The arrow flashed by, harmlessly slamming into one of the empty cupboards. The second vampire jumped at Fredrick, claws extended.

Sebastian swung his machete. He felt it connect on the vampire's upper arm. The impact was like smashing into a wall. It reverberated into his shoulders. The vampire wailed. It swung at Sebastian with its other arm. Sebastian ducked. His grip slipped on the machete. It was still embedded in the vampire's arm. The vampire lurched away, taking the machete with him.

Sebastian stumbled, grabbing for the handle. His foot twisted on the uneven floor and he crashed to his knees. The vampire slipped out of his reach, leaving Sebastian unarmed.

Oh shit!

From behind them, another vampire snarled, launching itself through the doorway from the hall. Sebastian heard the blast of the shotgun and the scream of one of the other men. In front of him, the vampire with the machete in its arm crouched and grinned at Sebastian.

It darted toward him. Sebastian jumped away, aiming for the window. His shoulder slammed into the wall. His hands scrabbled for purchase on the window covering. As he fell back to the floor, his grip tightened. The covering stretched, then ripped, falling away from the window.

Anaemic sunlight shone in. A headache stabbed into Sebastian's temples. The vampire screamed and scrambled away.

"The windows!" Sebastian shouted.

Over the screams and howls and shotgun blasts, he couldn't tell if anyone heard him. Fredrick shot an arrow into one of the vampires. It shuddered and fell, trying to dig the arrow out of its chest. Sebastian ran forward, grabbing its legs and dragged it farther into the light. It screamed and writhed as the sun hit it. Smoke began to drift from its clothes.

"Head!" Fredrick said. He slid a large knife along the floor toward Sebastian. Sebastian scooped it up just as another vampire lunged for it. Rolling on the floor, Sebastian used the momentum to slash upward.

The knife sliced upward through the vampire's torso, from its side up to its shoulder. It screamed, the edges of the injury smoking from the effects of the silver blade. It staggered away.

Sebastian jumped to his feet. He ran to the vampire writhing in the sunlight. He wished he had the machete. It would have made this so much easier. This knife was big but not big enough.

He slashed and stabbed, barely avoiding the vampire's claws that grabbed for him. At one point claws racked along his forearm, slicing into his skin. Sebastian cried out at the pain. He cut harder. The vampire's hands dropped, flopping on the floor. The head came away.

Sebastian grabbed it and flung it across the room. He heard the snarls and howls of other vampires. Several crouched in the doorway, out of reach of the strengthening sun. Sebastian saw Fredrick slumped against the kitchen counter, feebly trying to reload his crossbow. The other two men lay on the floor. From the blood, Sebastian could tell they were dead. He clutched the knife and shifted forward, aiming for one of the shotguns.

The vampire in the doorway hissed at him and darted forward. Sunlight sprayed across its back as it grabbed the shotgun and raced back to the doorway.

"You made a big mistake coming here, In-Between," it said to Sebastian. "We've got your scent now. We'll find you."

It raised the shotgun.

Sebastian grabbed Fredrick and lunged for the back door. They fell through the open doorway as the shotgun blasted. Sebastian felt tiny pellets strike his lower legs, tearing into his skin. Fredrick moaned. Sebastian saw the right sleeve of his shirt blossom with dots of red.

Pain ached in Sebastian's legs as he pulled Fredrick to his feet. He dragged them off to the side of the doorway, out of range of the shotgun.

"We have to go back," Fredrick said.

"We can't," Sebastian said. "You're out of arrows and the shotguns are back in there. The vampires have them. We have to get out of here. Your arm."

"Your legs."

Sebastian glanced down. His pants were soaked with blood from the knees down. He didn't feel it. Shock, adrenaline, whatever, he didn't want to be here when it wore off. He grabbed Fredrick's shirt.

"We have to go."

They stumbled away. Sebastian felt the edges of the wild grass sticking to his pants, almost reluctant to let go as he ran through it. Fredrick stumbled on ahead, finally breaking through to the road. The station wagon sat under the grove of trees. Fredrick began to move toward it.

Sebastian reached the road and stopped, bending to rest his hands on his thighs. He looked over at the station wagon. Funny, he didn't think they'd covered the windows.

"Fredrick, no!" he yelled.

Fredrick opened the door. A clawed arm slashed out. He jumped back, the claws missing him by an inch. The vampire inside hissed and retreated to hide in the back seat.

"We have to get it out of the car," Fredrick said.

Sebastian limped over. The lower part of his legs was starting to feel sticky from the blood but he didn't still didn't feel any pain. "How? It'll just lock the doors."

Fredrick hefted the crossbow. "We'll have to smash the windows. Back ones first."

Before Sebastian could say anything, the man stepped toward the back side window and swung. As the edge of the weapon hit the glass, he turned his head away. Sebastian turned his back. The window exploded inward. A snarl of rage sounded from inside. The creature snatched the blanket covering the window then darted out of the front door. It draped the blanket over its head and upper body. It snarled at them and fled, racing back to the house.

Fredrick approached the car with more caution but it was empty. He tossed the crossbow in the back seat and dropped into the driver's seat.

"Let's go."

Sebastian slid into the passenger's seat. "What about the others?"

"We head for the rendezvous," Fredrick said.

"But..."

"We follow orders. We head for the rendezvous."

He put the car in gear and hit the gas.

When they reached the main street, Fredrick turned left, heading back into Calais. Were they going back to the safe house? They both needed medical attention. Fredrick's right arm was soaked in blood. His hand trembled on the steering wheel. Although he still didn't feel anything Sebastian knew his legs were bad. He had no idea if he'd be able to stand up to get out of the car.

"We have to get help," he said.

"When we get there," Fredrick said.

"How long is that?" Sebastian said.

"Three, four hours."

"We can't last that long, not your arm and not my legs. We have to at least get some bandages."

"We wait until we get there."

The man sounded almost robotic. Sebastian recognized the symptoms of shock. Fredrick responded by going on automatic, following orders, no matter if those orders killed him. But they needed to stop.

How could he convince the man? His thoughts felt fuzzy, indistinct. His legs throbbed. Coming out of shock. Maybe moving into feeling the effects of blood loss. Would Fredrick feel it too? If he lost consciousness, they'd smash up and die on this road.

"Fredrick, what's the first priority of the In-Between?" Sebastian said.

"First priority is survival," Fredrick said.

"We aren't going to survive if we don't take care of our injuries right now. We've lost enough today, let's not lose ourselves."

Sebastian saw a flicker of movement in Fredrick's head, almost as if he turned toward Sebastian. At the next right, Fredrick signalled and turned off the main road.

"We'll find something down here."

He pulled up to the first house he saw. It was a small, two-story reddish-brown, brick house. Fredrick got out of the car. Sebastian opened the door on his side. He swung himself to face the door and put his feet on the ground. He felt his muscles tremble as he started to put weight on them. He hung onto the door and doorframe. Now his knees shook. He could almost feel the wounds start to bleed again. Get up, just a few steps, he promised his legs. They shook as if they didn't believe him.

By the time he reached the walkway to the door, Fredrick stood at the door, talking to a woman in the doorway. She already had the vacant, glazed expression of someone under the Influence of an In-Between. She opened the door wider to allow Fredrick to step inside. She held for the door for Sebastian as well. As he passed her, she stared straight ahead, not even seeing him.

The brown color of her hair reminded him of Jessica.

Had she survived... He pushed the thought away before he could even finish it. He didn't want to think about that, think about her. He'd lost everything and didn't think he could stand losing her as well. Not now.

He found Fredrick in the kitchen, a cheerful room painted bright yellow with lime green cabinets. The woman wandered in behind Sebastian.

"Bandages and ointment," Fredrick said. "A first aid kit if you have one."

She turned and left without even looking at him. Sebastian lowered himself onto the second chair at the small kitchen table across from Fredrick. The man cradled his right arm against his body.

"Is there anyone else here?" Sebastian said. He kept his voice down.

Fredrick nodded. "I think a husband and child. Still asleep. I hope I can keep them that way."

Sebastian opened his mouth but the woman returned. He didn't speak. Best to not do anything to place extra stress on the trance. Any audio sensory input was another piece that Fredrick had to block to keep her compliant and unaware of them.

She set a roll of bandages and a plastic box on the table. As she stepped back, Sebastian opened the box. It was a first aid kit. He found medical tape, ointment, extra bandages and even tiny scissors to cut the tape. He nodded to Fredrick.

"Go back to bed," Fredrick told the woman. "You deserve more sleep. You'll wake up in half an hour and feel refreshed."

"Hour," Sebastian whispered.

"An hour," Fredrick said. "Sleep for an extra hour."

The woman turned and left the room. Sebastian listened to her footsteps moving up the stairs then he started unwrapping the bandages.

"Your arm," he said to Fredrick.

He ended up cutting the shirt sleeve away and using a towel to wipe away the blood. He couldn't see any exit wounds. The pellets must still be in his arm, he thought.

"Just bandage it," Fredrick said. "We don't have time to dig the pellets out of my arm or your legs."

Sebastian nodded. After applying some ointment, he wrapped the bandage around Fredrick's forearm. Then Fredrick bent down to his legs.

"Your pants are stuck to your calves," Fredrick said. "It's gonna hurt."

"Go ahead," Sebastian said. He tightened his hands into fists on his lap.

Fredrick cut the pants away, peeling them off Sebastian's legs. He used the towel to wet down the stickier spots. Sebastian's fists tightened. He clenched his jaw, holding in the screams. He didn't want to wake anyone in the house.

Finally Fredrick finished and used the towel to wipe away the worst of the blood. A multitude of tiny holes dotted his calves. How could he even walk like that? As if hearing his thoughts, Fredrick lifted his head.

"You're an In-Between," he said. "We can take a lot worse punishment."

He applied ointment and wrapped the rest of the bandages around Sebastian's legs. Then he dumped the scissors into the box and shut it. He spread the towel on the table and gathered the remains of the shirt and Sebastian's pants into it. He picked up the box.

"Let's go," he said.

"Won't she miss the towel?" Sebastian said.

"Better for her to miss it than find blood all over it," Fredrick said.

They left the house, closing the door softly behind them. Fredrick tossed the first aid kit into the back seat then climbed into the driver's seat. As Sebastian got into the passenger's seat, Fredrick handed him the towel.

"We'll burn this later," Fredrick said.

They headed out into the rapidly developing daylight.

CHAPTER THREE

They drove the entire morning, then Fredrick stopped at a small bakery around eleven.

"Stay in the car," he said to Sebastian. "Your pants will draw attention." He pulled out a jacket from the backseat and slipped it on, hiding the bandage on his arm. He headed into the bakery.

Sebastian sat in the station wagon. The sun pounded on his head, adding to the throbbing in his legs. He'd tried to find out where they were going but only got monosyllabic answers from Fredrick. Did the man honestly think Sebastian was untrustworthy at this point? They didn't even know if anyone else had survived the raid.

He didn't even know if Jessica had survived.

He tried to push the worry down but it had been festering all morning and would no longer be denied. If he'd been in her team, he would have seen what happened to her. Her group had gone in through the front, far enough from the back that he hadn't been able see her. Again he cursed that he couldn't smell any In-Between and with so many people around and so much activity, he hadn't been able to feel her. Now he was assuming Fredrick was taking him to the rendezvous point where Jessica would also be heading.

If she survived.

She had survived. She had to, he wouldn't even consider otherwise. She was his final link to his regular life. Although he'd already been bitten when they met, he had still been living in his dorm with Charlie, Alexa had still been human, and for a few brief moments Sebastian had thought maybe he'd be able to have a normal life. But then the understanding of what had happened made him realize he'd never be normal again.

And Jessica had saved him from sinking completely.

Who knows, without her he might just have succumbed to Bianca or Constantine would have torn him apart.

He owed her something for that. He owed it to her to believe she survived. He would find her.

The driver's door opened, making him jump. Fredrick climbed in, tossing a bag onto Sebastian's lap.

"What's this?" Sebastian said.

Fredrick had his mouth full of pastry. "Croissants," came out garbled. "Eat."

The smell permeated the car before he even opened the bag. Too bad he couldn't taste them the same as he could smell them. After a year, he'd started to get used to the bland flavor of food. He still didn't like it but it didn't make him want to vomit anymore. He pulled out a croissant and handled the bag to Fredrick. Fredrick pulled out another one and stuffed it halfway into his mouth. He pulled the car out and into the street. His jaw chewed, pulling the croissant into his mouth.

"Are we going to the safe house now?" Sebastian said.

"Yeah." Fredrick nodded just in case Sebastian couldn't understand his food-mangled speech.

Sebastian made sure to eat at least a couple of croissants. Eating regular food at regular times was very important for the In-Between. It helped to stem the lure of blood and provided fuel for the body, even though they could go for several days without it. But if they went too long, they might succumb to the temptation of blood. Within the first month after a vampire attack, an In-Between 'solidified' into this state. He could never be turned into a vampire, but if he gave in to the temptation, if he drank blood, he would be turned into something else. Something crazed and craven that even the vampires didn't want to deal with.

Every time he didn't feel like eating, he thought of that. It always got him to take at least a few bites.

Fredrick turned down a narrow street and pulled up in front of an old, yellow brick building. As they got out of the car, Sebastian noticed it still had external fire escapes on its sides. Fredrick walked to the main door and pressed the buzzer multiple times. Three staccato beats and then two long. The door clicked open. He held it for Sebastian.

They trudged up the stairs. The cool air and dimness soothed Sebastian's head and loosened the muscles of his neck. Even after a year of adapting, he was still more sensitive than any of the other In-Between. He tried to hide it from them. They tended to be suspicious of anything outside their range of normal. But he couldn't ever hide it from Jessica. She'd always seemed to know when it was especially bothersome.

I'll find you.

They reached the fourth floor of the building. Fredrick led him down the hallway. Discolored, beige wallpaper covered the walls. Sebastian could smell the old glue barely holding the paper to the wall. The grey carpet beneath their feet was threadbare. At the fifth door on the right, Fredrick repeated the same rhythm as from the buzzer. Identification.

The door swung open, granting admission. Fredrick walked in. Sebastian followed. He caught a glimpse of a room to the right of the entrance way, empty except for two chairs, then something struck him on the back of the head.

Sebastian staggered and dropped to his knees. Fredrick stepped back as two men moved forward. They grabbed Sebastian's arms and dragged him into one of the chairs. His vision swam as they fastened his arms to the chair. They didn't bother with his legs.

Fredrick stepped in front of him. He held the paper bag in his hand. He pulled out a croissant and began to eat it.

Sebastian blinked until the two images of Fredrick coalesced into one. The back of his head ached. Three men other than Fredrick stood in the room, the two who had tied him to the chair and the third one who held a revolver in his hand. The butt end of it probably matched the indentation in the back of his skull.

"What is going on?" He managed to keep the words from slurring. Quite a feat.

Fredrick swallowed the final bit of his croissant. He handed the bag to one of the other men. He took the bag and poked around in it.

"You tell us," Fredrick said. "You went scouting with Nigel yesterday. He said there were six, you said thirteen. I'm wondering why the discrepancy."

Sebastian tilted his head. "I told you there were more vampires. Morgan decides to go in as if there are six and I'm the one being blamed for the discrepancy?"

"Morgan is dead," said the man holding the revolver.

Sebastian's mouth went dry. "Who else survived?"

The one holding the bag pulled out a croissant. "No one else has shown up."

Sebastian felt a coldness begin to creep into his veins and settle into his stomach. His stomach clenched against it.

Jessica...

"Yet," Sebastian said. "You mean yet. They might still be on the way."

Revolver man shook his head. "No calls. Protocol is they call."

"You destroyed our team," Fredrick said.

"You cannot be serious," Sebastian said. "Look at my legs. Do you think I sent you into a trap and allowed myself to get shot? I killed a vampire in there."

"That's why they shot you," Fredrick said. "You betrayed them just like you betrayed us."

Sebastian gaped at him. This couldn't be happening. They could not honestly believe he had anything to do with the disastrous raid...

The looks on their faces told him they did.

The coldness settled into his stomach, spreading poisonous fingers throughout his body. He bent over double. His hands clenched the arms of the chair. His feet sat flat on the floor.

"What's the matter with you?" Fredrick said.

"My... my stomach..."

Revolver man switched the revolver to his left hand as he stepped forward. He reached out a hand to Sebastian's forehead as if to feel his temperature.

Sebastian put his weight on his legs. He half stood, twisting to the left. He caught revolver man in the shoulder, knocking him down. One of the men shouted. Sebastian could have maintained his balance but then they would have thought he'd done it on purpose. He allowed momentum to carry him over. He fell to the floor, landing on the left side of the chair. The arm and one of the legs shattered. He slumped in the chair and then began to shake, as if convulsing.

Voices shouted around him. He kept his eyes closed to slits and shook his limbs. His left arm came free from the shattered chair arm. He started flapping it over his right arm, tugging at the rope, tugging.

"Get him up off the floor," Fredrick said. "Hurry up."

Sebastian felt arms trying to pick him up but being partially tied to the chair inhibited them. Finally one of them had to loosen the rope on his right arm...

He pressed his fingers together and jabbed the closest man in the throat. The man gurgled and fell back before anyone realized what had happened. Sebastian twisted and slammed his palm against another man's face. He felt the man's nose crunch under his hand. The man cried out, falling back.

Sebastian rolled as Fredrick made a grab for him. He ended up by a window in the wall. A sneer spread across Fredrick's face.

He blocked the only exit.

Sebastian went for the window.

He got half out before Fredrick realized what he was doing. He darted forward. Sebastian had his left leg inside, his right leg balanced on the ledge. Fredrick's hand closed on Sebastian's ankle. He yanked, dragging Sebastian's leg back into the room. Pain flared as Fredrick grabbed his calf. Sebastian let himself be pulled back into the room. He crumbled to the floor. Fredrick bent over him.

Sebastian grabbed the man's right forearm and twisted. Fredrick yelled in pain. Sebastian scrambled to his feet and shoved Fredrick hard. The man stumbled back, cradling his arm. He knocked into one of the other men and they tripped to the floor.

The men still blocked the path to the door.

The window. It was the only way.

Sebastian grabbed the edges of the window and hauled himself out. His toes hung over the end. Get moving. He started to edge his way along the ledge. Just to the right a few feet was the fire escape. He could just make it.

His left leg throbbed and shook from Fredrick's grab, slowing his progress. The sun blazed down, making his head pound. He squinted against it. A foot away from the fire escape, he saw another window leading back into the apartment. This room was a kitchen, long and narrow like a galley. The window frame gave him more handholds but the window itself was slippery and flat. He had to release the one side and hurry across to reach the other.

Steady, left leg. Just a little farther, then he'd be on the fire escape and away. He promised his leg a new bandage, a good soak in a tub, anything to stay strong and get him across this ledge to the fire escape.

He took a deep breath and started to creep forward.

Halfway across the window, he saw a shadow cross the doorway into the kitchen. One of the men looked in. The one he'd jabbed in the throat. His face flushed in anger. He ran across the room.

Sebastian hurried along the ledge. Three quarters there, four fifths there. The man reached the window and started lifting it. Sebastian felt the sliding top of the window scrap his thigh. He put his hand on it and shoved. It slammed down. His balance teetered. He dug his fingers into the sliding top. His other hand gripped the side of the window frame. His heart pounded in his chest. He felt like it might push him backward off the building. Stop that. Keep moving right.

His feet inched along again. Just before he fully passed the window, the man started sliding it open again. Sebastian hurried faster. He could almost reach the fire escape.

The window opened. The man reached out, grabbing the edge of Sebastian's pant leg. He yanked. Sebastian lurched to the right, trying to break the man's grip. For a moment, Sebastian teetered and then his foot slipped. He felt himself falling. He grabbed out to the right.

His hands caught the edge of the fire escape. He held on, feeling his body swing, the pressure snapping several fingernails. He used the swing to pull his right leg up. Pain raced up his leg as he banged the shin on the fire escape but he got his leg up. His breath hissed out of him as he struggled to pull himself upright and climbed over the railing.

He stumbled on the small landing. His fingers throbbed. He wanted to fall over and rest but he knew Fredrick and those men would be after him any minute now.

He started down the stairs two at a time.

Then stopped.

They would be expecting him to go down. With the elevator, they'd make it to the ground and could be waiting for him, hiding out of sight. The minute he reached the ground they'd be on him.

He turned and climbed up.

At the top floor, he tried the door. Locked. He pulled the tiny tool set from his back pocket. Jessica had given it to him when she'd taught him how to open locks. At first he hadn't wanted to learn something so criminal but he came to realize that his life was no longer so black and white. Grey washed out everything.

The tool set had been his graduation present at finally getting it right. Then she'd forced him to practice for hours to get the speed down.

Those hours had been boring as anything. He'd never had to use the skill but now he was grateful for the practice.

He wished he could show her how well he did.

His head pounding as he focused, he got the door open in under two minutes, his fastest time so far. Stepping into the darkened hallway was a relief after the sunshine. He limped down the hallway. He took a deep breath as he passed each door, trying to find a person inside. The first door held the faint hint of a person. Probably gone out. The second smelled the same but at the third, he caught the strong scent of heavy flowers inside. He would have to chance it.

He knocked and waited.

After a moment, he heard shuffling from inside. The door opened a few inches, then the chair pulled taunt. At the level of his chest, an old woman peeked out.

"Qui?"

Sebastian focused on her, allowed himself to hear her breathing, only her breathing and to match it. The bright alertness lingered in her eyes then her face slackened. Her eyes defocused.

"Open the door," he said in a monotone voice.

For a moment he worried that she didn't know English but then her hand reached up and unhooked the chain. She swung the door open. He limped inside.

"Shut and lock the door," he said.

She shut the door, reset the chain and twisted the bolt home. The inside of her apartment was decorated in pastels and puffiness as far as he could see. Even the throw pillows seemed overstuffed. The floral scent was thick and cloying, forcing him to breathe through his mouth.

"Do you have a car?" he said.

Her head shook from side to side. Of course, his luck wouldn't hold that well, he thought. At least he could re-bandage his legs here. The throbbing from his left one reminded him of his promise. Besides he could see blood seeping through the old bandage.

"Where is the kitchen?" he said to the old woman.

A heavily veined hand lifted and pointed to the right.

"Bring me bandages and some towels," he said. "Do you have any men's pants?"

She nodded. "Qui, yes. My son's."

"Bring me a pair of those too."

He limped into the kitchen. The old woman brought him everything a few moments later. He sent her off to the bedroom for a nap while he redressed his wounds. The pants turned out to be too wide at the waist and too short at the ankles but they were better than his ruined pair. His belt helped somewhat and after scrounging in the drawers, he found a few safety pins that secured them even more.

Now he had to find a way out of the building without running into Fredrick or his friends. Again he wished he could smell the In-Between, and he hadn't been around Fredrick enough to have gotten a good enough psychic impression of him. He'd only been around a few months. Sebastian thought he'd come as a favor to Morgan.

Through the back? That might be the exact spot they'd look for him. But the front was just as dangerous. It wouldn't take long for them to realize he hadn't left the building. They were bound to find him sooner or later.

The one good thing was that if he hadn't gotten a good impression of Fredrick, odds were the man hadn't gotten a good one of him either. They might both be operating blind.

He was going to have to chance the front door. Unfortunately for that, he'd need a shield.

He found the old woman in the bedroom and tapped on the inside of the door frame to catch her attention. She looked startled to see him but soon the defocused look came back into her eyes.

He had her fetch a coat and her purse for a walk to the fruit market down the street. She seemed to think he was her son and even took his arm. He let her. Any action that made her more comfortable kept her in the trance and under his Influence longer.

Before they left, he did have to remind her to lock the door.

The elevator ride was tense for him until they passed the fourth floor, then he relaxed. So far so good. They might make it to the street. If he could get a block or two away, he could disappear.

They managed half a block.

The sun shone right down on them and he was squinting when he noticed the man across the street with hunched shoulders. Something about him... He turned and Sebastian recognized him. Revolver man.

"You get yourself some nice fruit and head home," he told the old woman. "Never mind me. You don't remember anyone with you at all."

"All right," she said.

He slid his arm out from hers just as they passed an alley. She walked on and he ducked inside.

His feet pounded the asphalt. For a moment, his steps were the only ones he heard, then he heard another set following him. He chanced a glance back.

Revolver man.

Sebastian ran hard. His legs ached with each step. He could feel the pull of the bandages but so far he hadn't bled through again. But he would and he wouldn't be able to keep up this pace for long.

He had to lose the man chasing him.

The alley crossed another street. Sebastian turned right. More pedestrians walked along this street. He dodged in and out of them. They slowed his progress but he knew they slowed his pursuer as well.

The pounding of his feet echoed the pounding of his heart. His lungs felt like they would burst. Now the pain in his lower legs throbbed. The pull of the bandages made it worse. He had to be bleeding again. Damn good thing it wasn't night, his blood would draw the vampires for miles. Too bad he was poison to them now.

A small consolation when they could still rip out his throat.

He reached the corner just as the light turned red. He thundered forward, right into the path of a car. It missed him by an inch, horn blaring. Tires screeched and swearing in French followed him. As he reached the other side and crossed the other way, he heard more shrieking and cursing. His pursuer had decided to be reckless too.

Dammit.

Then as he reached the other side of the street he spotted salvation two cars lengths down. A taxi! He put on a burst of speed. Pain shot up his legs. He stumbled just as he reached the taxi. A woman moved in front of him, opening the back door to enter.

"This is my taxi," he said. He fought to keep his voice steady.

"Pardon moi." The woman turned with a frown. He locked eyes with her. Her hand dropped from the door handle. She stepped back.

Sebastian dove into the back seat. "Drive!" He pushed all his energy behind the command.

The taxi jumped into traffic just as revolver man reached the door. He grabbed for the handle, bumping the woman. She turned and swung at him with her purse. He lifted his arm to block the purse and lost his grip on the door. As the taxi pulled away, he stumbled and tripped into the street. The woman stood there shouting at him.

Sebastian watched the whole thing from the back window then turned back to the driver.

"Head south," he said.

It was the first thing he thought of.

***

He dozed in the back seat and woke when they reached Rouen. The driver appeared ready to keep going but Sebastian stopped him. He realized he had a little over one hundred and fifty euros. He had the driver pull over beside a small bed and breakfast. He pulled out two five euro notes and pressed them into the man's hands.

"You earned every penny of this five hundred euros," he said.

The man's eyes widened. He started to sputter and almost pushed them back at Sebastian.

"No keep them, I insist." Before the man could protest further, Sebastian got out of the car. The man shouted his thanks through the open window and drove off. Sebastian waved and watched him drive off before turning to the bed and breakfast.

The drive had stiffened his legs. It took all his strength not to limp up the walk way to the front desk. Another five euros earned him a great smile from the proprietor who, also believing it was five hundred, ushered him up the stairs. He followed her slowly, trying not to groan. She stood practically vibrating at the top of the stairs and then led him all the way down the hall to the final bedroom on the left. She handed him a single key and left, not noticing or commenting on his lack of luggage.

He'd almost asked for more bandages but he didn't think he had the concentration to make her forget that. His brain felt almost stretched out of shape from having to Influence so many people. He'd never had to do that before. It was a wonder he wasn't bleeding from his ears.

He stumbled into the tiny bathroom off the bedroom. His face looked pale and drawn, his hair limp, but no blood from his ears. He saw a small shower but no tub. He wouldn't be able to soak his legs after all. He considered trying to take a shower to wash his legs or sleep first.

Sleep won.

He limped back into the bedroom and pulled the shades shut. Then he fell into bed, pulling the sheets over his head to block out more of the sun.

This was the first time he'd been on his own since he'd joined the In-Between.

Was that a bad thing?

CHAPTER FOUR

Darkness filled the room when he woke up. For a moment, he didn't know where he was or why the covers were over his head. For a moment, he was back to his dorm room with Charlie and the first few days of being an In-Between. He hadn't even know what that was at the time, just that he couldn't stand the sun and lying with the covers over his head made it that much harder for the sun to reach him.

But pushing the covers down shattered the moment. It wasn't his dorm room and Charlie wasn't sitting across the room on his single bed.

Charlie wasn't even alive anymore.

With the dark came more energy. When he stood and crossed the bedroom, he didn't limp. His legs still ached but it was a dull pain as if they were more annoyed than anything.

After a quick shower, he noticed small bumps on his lower legs. He sat on the toilet and lifted one onto the sink. He squeezed at the bump and out popped a piece of silver shot. It was as if his legs were pushing them out of his body. He'd known he could heal faster from wounds. Even the scrape across his forearm was almost healed, but he'd never had an injury like this. He'd never imagined it would heal this fast.

He popped out several more that were close to the surface. Others still seemed farther in so he left them. His legs ached a little bit from it but it felt different now. He could tell he'd turned some corner.

The sleep had done him a world of good.

So now what? Should he try to connect with another group of In-Between? It sounded like his team had been decimated by the disastrous raid. Would Fredrick and his friends spread rumors about him betraying them? He didn't know enough about how the In-Between communicated. There was some contact through the forums that Charlie's friend Stan had discovered but they were used sporadically, more to draw in any stray In-Between who may have been infected and was alone.

Like he was now.

He was alone. For the first time since he'd become an In-Between, he was alone. He pulled his leg off the sink and set it on the floor. He looked around the small bathroom. Here he was, alone in Europe. He always imagined he'd visit here but never like this. Often he'd thought he and Charlie would backpack across Europe after college, before they each got jobs. Sometimes that fantasy had even included Alexa and in his deepest dreams, he sometimes imagined it was just the two of them, together, and they would fall in love under the Paris lights.

God, they felt like dreams from a century ago, dreams of a child. Had he ever been that young? He felt like he'd aged more in a year than in his whole life until then. But now he was alone.

Now he was free.

He didn't have to go back to the other In-Between if he didn't want to, didn't have to sign up for their never-ending war against the vampires and live from skirmish to skirmish. He could find some other way to live.

Freedom.

He felt his whole body trembling as he returned to the bedroom. He'd never given any consideration to being on his own while he was with the In-Between. They made it sound like it was dangerous, being surrounded by regular people, always smelling their blood. An overwhelming temptation. But maybe if he found a small town. He could live on the outskirts, come in only occasionally. He could limit his exposure to regular people, maybe even build up a tolerance. Living with the In-Between was almost like a self-fulfilling prophecy, they said it couldn't be done and it couldn't be, not when he was surrounded by them.

But maybe he could do it on his own.

It would be a big challenge, he knew that. He seemed to be more sensitive than the other In-Between in many ways, more sensitive to the sun, more sensitive to call of blood. Over the past year he'd become more accustomed to the sun, even if it did hurt. He was able to resist the scent of blood as long as he remembered to eat food and rested enough.

It would take some work. He knew that. But he was going to try.

His heart pounded with excitement. He grinned at the room around him. His first night alone. His first step into a new life!

What about Jessica, a small voice inside him asked.

He sat down heavy on the bed.

He'd forgotten about her.

How could he do that? She'd done everything to help him and asked nothing in return. He didn't even know if she was alive. With no connection to the In-Between, would he ever be able to find out? He knew she had a central voicemail, maybe he could leave her a message and a number she could call. Something that couldn't be traced.

He dressed quickly and rubbed a towel through his hair. When he pulled back the drapes, he realized it wasn't quite sundown although the sun was low in the sky. He checked the time. Quarter after eight, almost sundown. He could venture out and maybe find some place where he could buy an untraceable phone.

That should be easy, right?

Now that he'd had some rest, it should be a little easier.

He started with the proprietor. A gentle nudge gave him the name of her uncle's old friend who ran an appliance store a few blocks away. From her tone, he gathered there might be some questionable activities by this friend. Perfect for him.

As he turned to leave, she pushed a jacket on him, telling him it was too cold for his shirt. He took it without arguing. It was always best not to contradict someone when he Influenced them.

Outside the air did hold a touch of chill so he slipped the brown jacket on. It was a little tight across the shoulders but all right as long as he didn't bend forward.

A few people strolled the street with him. He could smell them all and even tell where they were positioned. With a good sleep came an increased sensitivity. Of course, he wasn't running for his life now either.

He smelled a young couple behind him. Her laugh was a trickle in his ear. Even their walk was a study in new love; their footsteps matched step by step. He could almost smell their pheromones in the air.

He jumped into the street and hurried across, cutting off a truck that blared its horn at him. The driver shouted in French, shaking his head. Sebastian gave him an apologetic wave as he reached the other sidewalk.

He couldn't stand sensing that young couple behind him. It reminded him too much of Alexa, too much of the dreams he'd once had that could never happen.

He didn't need to be reminded.

He followed the proprietor's directions and found the store a few blocks farther down. More people wandered here where a number of cafés dotted the street, extending patios onto the sidewalk. Chattering voices filled the air, underscored by music playing inside the cafés. Regular human nightlife, he'd almost forgotten what it was like. How wonderful would it be to sit on one of those patios, sipping a glass of wine, watching the night unfold as people walked by? His footsteps slowed as he passed another patio. They even had a free table. The perfect size for one. He could sit there and inhale the scent of blood around him...

Stop!

He hurried past.

He couldn't do that yet. Maybe not ever. When he found his own place out somewhere in the country, away from people, then he could sit outside and watch the night come. But not now, not here.

Just get a damned phone.

He found the shop two doors down. The closed sign was already on the door but it swung lazily, as if someone had just turned it. He knocked on the door. Nothing. He knocked again and kept knocking. Finally he heard a shuffling come from the back. He kept knocking. A mumbled curse followed the shuffling as they got closer to the door.

"Closed!" An older man appeared at the door, pointing at the sign.

"Madame Lenore sent me here," Sebastian said.

The man's frown didn't lessen as he pursed his lips. Sebastian pulled a five euro note from his pocket and held it close to his chest. He sent the image of a five hundred euro note to the man. His eyes widened.

"Qui, of course, come in!" His hands fumbled on the door latch in their haste to open the door.

Sebastian stepped into the cool darkness of the shop. He breathed in the tang of electrical components and dust in the carpeting. The older man, now seeming not much older than fifty when seen up close, folded his hands in front of him.

"Any friend of Madame Lenore is welcome here. What can I get for you, sir?"

"I need a prepaid cell phone, untraceable," Sebastian said. "No, make that... three of them. Different numbers all."

"I see." The man bowed his head and tapped his lip. "This is quite the request, sir."

"I'll double the amount you saw," Sebastian said.

The man's head snapped up. "Of course, this way."

He ushered Sebastian to the back of the store. He made to turn on the light but stopped at Sebastian's shake of his head. The man obviously knew every nook and cranny in his shop and Sebastian could see fine in the dark.

They passed the counter and the man led him into the back room. When the door closed behind him, the man turned on a small yellow light, revealing a cramped room cluttered with boxes stacked almost as high as the top of Sebastian's head. Now that had to be illegal, he thought, eyeing a box that sagged to one side. He moved a step away from that one.

The man poked in a box under the work bench and then pulled out three phones. He removed them from their packaging and opened the back. He laid them out like an assembly line and set to work putting them each together, first the SIM card, then the battery, then registering them on the small laptop sitting at the end of the work bench.

"You have a name for the number?" the man said.

"John Smith," Sebastian said.

The man nodded and smirked. He turned back to his computer. It took him another ten minutes to finish setting up the phones, then he slid them across the work bench to Sebastian.

"All done," the man said. He jotted down the phone numbers for each phone and handed the slip of paper to Sebastian. Each phone was a different make and the man had matched the model to the number. Efficient, he'd done something like this before. Sebastian almost felt bad about ripping the man off.

Almost.

He stuffed the phones into his pants pockets. Not an attractive look, he thought. Then he pulled out the two five euro notes and placed them on the work bench. The man looked at them, hunger plain on his face.

"You found this money on the street," Sebastian said. "You've had no customers tonight."

The smile on the man's face faded. His hand that had been reaching for the notes flopped on the work bench. His eyes defocused as a slack expression came over his face.

"You've been alone this evening," Sebastian repeated. He wanted to make sure the command stuck.

"Alone," the man said. His voice slurred.

Sebastian backed away, maintaining eye contact until he bumped against the door. He groped for the door knob behind him then pushed the door open. He slipped through into the darkness and closed the door.

He hurried to the front and watched until no one was within close sight of the door, then he slid out. He pulled the front door shut. He didn't have the ability to lock it and didn't want anyone to notice him leaving. The man might not venture to the front of the store right away. Sebastian didn't want anyone to steal anything from him.

He headed off, away from the direction of his bed and breakfast.

He didn't want to be near it, just in case. Over the past year, he found himself becoming more and more paranoid. It was a fact of life as an In-Between.

Using his sense of smell, he found a small parkette off one of the side streets several blocks away. In the center, an old fountain sat dry. Odd that it wasn't working. He found a bench set farther back, under the shade of a tree and beside a large bush. He fished out the first phone and turned it on.

It showed minimal battery life but it was enough for him to make one call. He'd recharge it when he got back to the bed and breakfast.

He dialled Jessica's number by heart and pressed the phone to his ear. Her voice sounded like she was just standing next to him.

"You've reached my personal voice mail. If you've gotten this number, you know I'll call you back if I can. Leave a message."

For a moment, his throat tightened with the ache of hearing her voice. Would he ever hear it in person again? Yes, he would, dammit. He would!

"Jessica, it's me," he said. "I made it through the raid. Listen, I don't care what any of them say, you know me. You know I wouldn't betray you. I told Nigel I sensed thirteen in the house but he insisted on telling Morgan what he sensed. They didn't listen to me, but I want you to. I want you to call me. I have to talk to you. Please Jessica."

He read off the number for the phone then hung on a moment longer, not sure what else to say. Finally, he ended up, "I hope you're okay. Call me."

Then he hung up.

He stuffed the phone in his left pocket. He'd have to charge that one as soon as he got back to the bed and breakfast. He knew he should head back there now but night had fallen around him, sinking the parkette into shadows. As usual, he felt the contentment and power of the night energize him. The sounds of night creatures chirping and rustling in the grass and trees sounded around him. After all the sleep, he couldn't just head back to his room. His body almost vibrated now. He needed a good long walk around the city, maybe even case out a few places for potential sources of money. He couldn't expect his current stash to last forever.

He pushed off from the bench. His body seemed to flow in the night, moving with a gliding grace he would never have dreamed of when he was still fully human. The cooling air tingled on his skin. He breathed in the fresh scent of the grass and pollen from the trees. April in France was a riot of spring with everything bursting with new growth. He never got a chance to appreciate it.

He walked the perimeter of the parkette, letting the leaves of bushes brush against his arms, touching the trunks of the trees, feeling the rough texture tug at his fingertips. Even off the path in the near total darkness, he could see the detailed ridges of branches as they jutted out from the trunks. How did they know which direction to grow in, he'd always wondered. How did the tree know the best way to the sun? He pressed his cheek to the trunk and felt its rough texture scrap his skin.

The sound of a trickling laugh caught his attention. A woman. Footsteps sounded on the path toward the empty fountain. He turned to see a couple strolling arm in arm toward the fountain, scouting for a bench. Long blond hair flowed over the woman's shoulders. Her head tipped back as she laughed at something the man said. He smiled, his hand sweeping out to gesture at a bench around the opposite side of the fountain. They moved that way, disappearing around the fountain. He lost sight of them completely as they sat down.

A pair of lovers enjoying a private space. No one else came here to this empty fountain. He should leave them alone. They deserved their privacy.

But when his feet moved, it wasn't to leave the parkette, it was to carry him to the right, circling the fountain so he could get a better vantage point.

What the hell was he doing? He wasn't a peeping tom but when he caught sight of them again, he stopped and watched. They were now sitting on the bench, embracing and kissing. A flush warmed Sebastian's face. What was he doing, he wondered vaguely but part of him already knew. He felt an ache in his chest, watching this couple do something he'd never be able to do. How could he ever relax with a woman like that? The scent of her blood so close would overwhelm him.

Who was he kidding thinking he could live a normal life? This in front of him was a normal life and he'd never be able to have it. Okay, maybe not this but there were still other things he could do. He didn't have to live a war.

Enough. He had to stop torturing himself. These people deserved their privacy. He turned to step away, to sink deeper into the shadows of the parkette and leave when the breeze tickled his nostrils, bringing him the scent of the woman's perfume, and a thick sour stench.

He spun back in time to see the man's mouth open as he bent over the woman's neck.

He raced forward. Grabbing the man's shoulder, he wrenched back, yanking the man off the woman. He recognized the dazed, unfocused look of someone under vampiric influence.

"Wake up," he shouted in her face. "Run!"

She blinked at him, looking confused but he didn't have time to deal with her.

The vampire snarled and slashed out at Sebastian. Thick claws missed his shirt by bare inches. Sebastian dodged back, settling into a defensive crouch, his arms positioned at ready. It suddenly occurred to him he had no weapons of any kind. No holy water, no garlic, no stake.

What the hell was he doing facing a vampire at night?

Apparently the vampire noticed and wondered the same thing. A wolfish smile curled his lips, revealing his fangs.

"It's impolite to interrupt," the vampire said. "You should really wait your turn."

He lunged partway through his last sentence but Sebastian was ready. The vampire telegraphed all his moves, allowing Sebastian to dart away and stay just out of range. He backed around the fountain, using it as a partial cover. It also allowed him to move the vampire a little farther away from the girl.

"I'm getting tired of dancing with you," the vampire said. "I have a dinner to attend to."

He started to turn away.

Sebastian darted sideways, into the grove of trees. The vampire dashed after him. They ran through the trees. Sebastian grabbed at small branches, tearing them away. Too flimsy. As he dodged a bush, the vampire grabbed for him, catching one foot and off balancing him.

Sebastian tumbled, turning it into a roll but the precious moments allowed the vampire to catch up. It pounced on him.

Sickly sour breath filled Sebastian's nostrils making him gag. The vampire made to bite him, then reared back. A snarl twisted his mouth.

"In-Between! You mean to poison me!" The vampire's nails dug into Sebastian's shoulders. "I'll take care of you."

One hand closed on Sebastian's neck, tightening. Claws scrapped his skin. He felt the hand closing off his air way. Sebastian's mouth gaped open. He tried to pull in air. Pressure built up in his chest. His forehead tingled. His skin tightened on his scalp. He thought he saw dust particles flashing in front of his eyes. One hand clawed at the vampire's hand, trying to break the iron grip. The vampire chuckled and the sound reverberated in Sebastian's head. It would be the last thing he ever heard...

His other hand groped on the ground, grabbing grass, dirt, leaves, a branch...

A branch.

Hand clenched. His arm swung and he stabbed upward, shoving hard. For the briefest moment, the vampire's chest resisted, then the skin parted under the power of Sebastian's near-vampire strength. The vampire shrieked, rearing up away from Sebastian.

Gone! The hand gone! Sebastian sucked in air, coughing. He rolled to his side. The vampire staggered back, both hands on the tree branch, trying to pull it out of his chest.

Must have missed the heart full on. Sebastian climbed to his feet. As air filled his lungs, strength flowed back into his limbs. He stepped toward the vampire. A twist of that branch and he could pierce the bastard's heart.

The same thought must have occurred to the vampire. It hissed at him and backed away, still tugging at the branch. Finally it yanked the branch free and whipped it away. The branch spun off into the darkness. Sebastian glanced over to see where it landed. Too far for him to chase without the vampire catching up.

But this vampire seemed to have other plans. One hand clutched at the hole in its chest as it glared at him.

"You will pay for this, freak," he said. "My master Kobol will make you pay dearly before you die. Just try to run. It'll make it more fun for him and you won't stop us."

The vampire retreated, then turned and sped off into the night.

Sebastian glanced around the parkette. The girl had vanished, probably run off during the fight. Good thing, what she'd have witnessed might have driven her mad.

No one needed to know nightmares were real if they didn't have to.

As a precaution, he gathered another branch, smaller, concealable in his sleeve and as he left the parkette, he wondered.

Who the hell was Kobol?

CHAPTER FIVE

Sebastian grabbed some takeout food and headed back to the bed and breakfast. Only when he got to his room did he realize why the counter girl had been looking at him oddly. Blood dotted the front of his shirt. The vampire. Dammit.

Could he never *not* spill something on his shirt?

Tomorrow he had to get more clothes. He stripped the shirt off and dumped it in the bathroom sink. He rubbed soap into the stains and left it soaking in cold water as he returned to the food.

He still found eating to be annoying and sometimes nauseating but he realized the necessity of it. Eating food gave his body energy and kept him just one more step away from being a vampire. Compared to the other In-Between he'd met, his steps were quite a bit shorter than theirs. Probably the main reason why they didn't trust him.

Sometimes he wasn't sure he trusted himself.

He used the plastic fork and ate the curry while he stood by the window. The night still reigned outside but he could feel the dawn coming. It prickled on his scalp and tingled up his spine, almost a call of danger, get out of sight. None of the other In-Between seemed to sense the sun so early.

Oh good, let's recite the entire litany of how different he was from them.

Stop it.

It just covered up his real issue, which was the fear of how close he was to being a vampire. How much more time had Bianca needed to feed on him before he'd turned? Another few minutes? Another minute? Maybe just another mouthful?

He still had nightmares about her coming to finish the job. He didn't tell anyone about them, not even Jessica. But it didn't matter, she always seemed to know. She never said anything but he would find her silver knife lying on his pillow that night. He would sleep with it under the pillow and it always seemed to comfort him. Just having a weapon in case eased his mind and the dream would fade. In the morning he would return the blade to her and she'd take it from him without saying a word.

Maybe she'd be able to tell him who Kobol was.

Another reason why he wished she would call.

He pulled out the phone and checked it. The power was dead. Shit! He'd been out too long and the meager power had faded. He plugged it in and turned the phone on. No message. His shoulders drooped.

She hadn't called yet.

Leave it. Staring at the phone wouldn't make her call faster. He returned to the curry. Like all food, even at its spiciest, he couldn't taste a thing. It was just bland mush. He managed to eat several more bites before his stomach started to grumble. Well, at least he'd manage over half of it. Pretty good for him.

He dumped it in the garbage and checked on the shirt. The stains looked a little faded but it was hard to tell with the fabric soaking. He rinsed it in cold water and rung it out. Then he hung it over the shower. Hopefully it would be dry enough in a few hours for him to wear it out shopping for more clothes.

A check of the phone showed him it hadn't rung while he'd been in the bathroom, about twenty feet away. Oh, he wasn't impatient, no. What the hell was she doing? Oh probably running for her life, maybe trying to help others run for their lives, but you'd think she'd find time to check her voice mail.

Sebastian, you are losing it.

He sank down on the bed and lay with his arms under his head as he stared up at the ceiling. So now what? By tomorrow the phone would be charged enough that he could carry it while shopping for clothes, but what was the next move? He had to have some idea, especially when Jessica called him back (and she would call him back).

The idea of finding some little house outside a small town still appealed to him. No more vampires. No more In-Between. He yearned for as normal a life as possible, even if he did end up spending most of the nights awake and slept during the days. He closed his eyes, envisioning a small bungalow style house. Funny that the carpeting looked close to what he'd had at home growing up...

His breath deepened as he slipped into sleep. His daydream blended into a sleep dream. The carpeting from childhood was soon accompanied by furniture from his childhood, most of it long gone before he left for college. It somehow seemed perfectly reasonable for the decor to be this way. He moved from room to room, recognizing the pieces. That desk had been his mother's, that wardrobe had been his father's. He stepped into the living room and found Jessica sitting on the floral couch from when he was five. She held an old leather-bound book in her hand. Her ever-present ponytail draped over her left shoulder and it shifted as she looked up at him.

"Hello darling," she said. "Would you like some coffee?"

"Sure," he said.

She set the book on the coffee table (his grandmother's that he used to chase his brother around when they visited her). As she passed him, her hand squeezed his bicep and she brushed his cheek with her lips. His skin tingled from their soft warmth.

She headed into the kitchen. He turned to look at the book. The leather had an odd look to it, a paler color than he would have expected. The front curled just a little. His hand reached for it. He touched the spine, nudging the book. It shifted on the surface of the coffee table, leaving some kind of smear behind. His heart hammered in his chest.

His grandmother would be so angry about her coffee table! She didn't like him making a mess. She always scolded him for spilling things over everything, especially over himself.

But wait, this was *his* house. He didn't have to worry about her reaction anymore. Instead of slowing down, his heart sped up. It wasn't just the coffee table, it was something about that smear, that deep red smear.

"Here's your coffee, honey." Jessica spoke from behind him.

He straightened and turned. She handed him a sippy cup.

"Now don't spill it and drink it all up."

"Thanks," he said. He lifted the cup.

Before he could take a sip, the doorbell rang. Jessica smiled at him. "I'll get it."

She turned, her pony tail whipped around and swayed from side to side as she walked to the door, mimicking the sway of her hips. She paused at the door, hand on the door knob, and glanced over her shoulder at him.

"Aren't you naughty," she said. "Drink it all up."

He smiled and lifted the cup to his lips. Jessica opened the door. Sebastian took his first swallow. From the darkness outside, a robed figure stepped through the doorway. Jessica stepped back to let it enter.

Instead of the bitterness of coffee, Sebastian tasted a thick, iron flavor on his tongue. He shouldn't be able to taste anything. One swallow and he lowered the sippy cup. Sure enough, a drop lingered on the lip and then fell, falling in slow motion to land smack on the center of his shirt. As he watched, a stain spread across the front of his shirt, expanding from a tiny dot to cover over half the shirt and still it spread its red, oozy liquid over the fabric.

Sebastian wiped his mouth and saw red on his hand. Standing by the door, Jessica smiled at him, her fangs reflected light.

"Say hello to our guest," she said.

The robed figure glided forward. Sebastian felt a coldness sweep over him. He tried to open his mouth to speak but he couldn't move. Claws gripped his arms. The hood of the robe drifted toward his face. A sour stench filled his nostrils. He saw a glint of fangs reflecting the light from the overhead lamp.

"I am Kobol," a voice roared in his ears and in his mind. "Give me the book!"

A mouth closed on his neck and ripped out his throat while ringing...

⚜

Sebastian jolted awake. What? Where? The unfamiliar room swirled around him as he looked around. The ringing screeched in his ear. A phone. He saw it on the nightstand and grabbed it. As his fingers closed around it, memory flooded back. The raid, Fredrick's accusations, running, the room, calling Jessica.

Jessica!

An image of fangs in her mouth flashed into his mind and then was gone as he hit the answer button and lifted the phone to his ear.

"Yes?"

"Sebastian!" Her voice sounded muffled over the line, as if she was trying to keep it down. "Don't tell me where you are."

"Jessica, where are you? Are you okay?"

"Yes, I'm... yes, good enough. Fine. Just some scratches," she said. "Only three of us on our team made it out. Two of the other teams haven't reported in yet. We think they might all be gone. Sebastian, it was a disaster."

His stomach tightened at her news. Two teams lost, eight or more people.

"They're blaming you, Sebastian." Her voice dipped even lower. "Nigel's saying you called in the extra vampires."

"That's ridiculous," he said. "I told Nigel there were thirteen, I told Morgan."

"Morgan's dead," she said. "The others are scared. It's easier to blame you because you're the new one."

"Right, and I didn't fit in," he said. "So it must be me."

"I know it isn't you," she said.

Her affirmation loosed the knot in his stomach. A flood of relief washed over him. He wished she was here now in the room, not over the phone who knew where.

"They'll figure that out too eventually," she said. "But for now you need to just stay away. Keep your head down. I'll call you again with some instructions on how to pick up some money so you can stay off the grid for a while."

"Don't worry about that," he said. "I can get money."

"Okay," she said.

He sensed she was going to hang up but he didn't want to let her go, not yet. He had to find something else to say, some way to keep her talking.

"I stopped a vampire earlier. Missed the heart though. He was able to pull the branch I shoved in him out of his chest."

She snorted a laugh over the phone. "You have to hit the heart. It isn't as easy as it sounds."

"I know," he said. "He told me his master Kobol would get me."

Silence on the phone line. He couldn't even hear her breathing. Had she hung up on him?

"Jessica? Are you there?"

"Who... who did you say?" Her breath was a faint whisper.

"Kobol," he said. "Who is that?"

"You really believe in getting noticed from the top, don't you?" she said. "Kobol is Constantine's blood sibling and head of a rival clan." A choked laugh sounded over the phone. "Can't you keep your head down for a minute?"

"Well, the vampire was attacking this girl," he said. "What was I supposed to do? Walk away?"

"Without back up or help? Yes," she said.

"And let the girl die?"

"If necessary, yes."

He shook his head even though she couldn't see him over the phone. "I can't do that."

"And that is your problem right there."

From any of the other In-Between he would have bristled, but he could almost hear the smile in her voice and could even picture it in his head, the slight upturn of her lips and the narrowing of her eyes as she shook her head at him. She was forever chastising him to be more ruthless but he couldn't. He had the impression that she didn't really want him to change but had to say it because of the other In-Between.

"So what do I do?" he said.

"Stay put. I'll call again in a couple of hours. You didn't put your name on this cell or anything?" she said.

"No," he said. "I acquired it from a man who won't remember."

"Good. I'll call you in three hours."

She hung up before he could say anything else. She hadn't even asked him where he was but then he realized she probably didn't want the other In-Between to know. She was probably going to spend the next three hours finding a way to get away from them so she could call him with more privacy.

As for him, he should probably take care of that shopping.

After a quick shower, he headed out and his first purchase was a pair of sunglasses to combat the bright sunlight. The day had dawned blindingly clear, sending a pounding headache through his skull. Without any Octenphotohistra, the sun bothered him almost as much as when he first became an In-Between. He was just more used to it now. Although it did encourage a briefer shopping excursion.

He found a men's casual clothing store and bought half a dozen plain t-shirts, two long sleeve shirts and three pairs of jeans. As the clerk wrapped everything and piled it into a large paper bag, Sebastian handed over two ten euro notes, Influencing him to see two five hundred euro notes. The man scrambled to make enough change. He almost cleaned out the register and still "owed" Sebastian fifty euros.

"Keep it," Sebastian told the clerk as he took the bag.

"Oh merci, thank you, sir!"

He waved with such unbridled enthusiasm as Sebastian left the store that Sebastian felt a bit guilty about it. He didn't like Influencing people to steal from them but he needed to replenish his reserves.

By the time he returned to his room, his cell phone was ringing. He dumped the bag on the bed and shut the door, locking it before he answered.

"Okay, I slipped away," Jessica said. "I changed direction three times and cars twice. They aren't following me. Now where are you?"

He opened his mouth then stopped. He wanted to just tell her but he couldn't be sure if she was as clear as she thought. Maybe they'd even put her up to calling again. He couldn't risk it no matter how much he wanted to.

"I'll meet you at ten tonight at the Pont Des Arts bridge over the Seine," he said.

She burst out laughing. "Good! I'm glad to see some of it is sinking in. I'll be there for ten."

He felt his chest puff up with pride as she hung up.

She was actually coming here. He hadn't expected that. All he'd hoped for was to stay in touch by phone with the occasional clandestine call. With the other In-Between no longer trusting him, he knew he'd be a pariah no matter where he went. None of the other cells would have anything to do with him once the story of the raid got out. Nigel would be sure to twist it to blame him. He figured Jessica would want to stay in the loop. But coming to meet him... He knew that would cost her a lot.

He spent the rest of the day resting up and was scouting the proper spot by nine-thirty. He'd had to stop himself from getting there any earlier. It would have looked really out of place for him to be wandering around for over an hour. As it was, he could pretend to be looking at the river and such for half an hour. That wasn't too far outside the realm of possibility.

Just before ten a taxi pulled up, stopping several feet away. The back door swung up and Jessica stepped up. She smiled and nodded, her ponytail bobbing behind her.

The urge to run to her made him dart forward a few paces until he stopped himself and slowed to a casual walk. Her lips pursed and amusement twinkled in her eyes. She slung her backpack over her shoulder and slammed the car door shut. As the taxi pulled away, he reached her. She tilted her head as she scrutinized him.

"You don't look any worse for wear," she said.

He noticed the fading bruise along the hairline above her left temple. She stood in a way that favored her right hip.

Looked like they'd both come away with a little damage.

"I got silver shot on my shins and slashed on my forearm." He pulled up his right sleeve to show her the healing scrapes. Her smile faded a little as her eyebrows drew together in concern.

"You okay?" she said.

"Yeah, should be fine in another few days." He lifted his hand and touched the bruise on her head with his fingertips. "Looks like you got your share."

She shrugged. "The vamp who did it got worse."

He hesitated, then dropped his hand away. He'd wanted to trace the line of her cheek and jaw, to feel the realness of her, but let it go.

She was here and that was enough.

He turned to lead her away from the river. "I'm at a little bed and breakfast. It's only got one bed but we can find somewhere else."

"I only managed to access a few hundred euros," she said. "We'll have to ration. I don't mind the floor."

He would not let her take the floor but he knew well enough than to argue it at that moment.

When they reached his room, she walked into the center, nodding her approval. She checked out the window sites, the location of the bed and furniture and the bathroom setup. Finally, she tossed her backpack onto the chair by the window.

"Good choice," she said. "Decent coverage of the street. No direct sightline to the room. Bed angled away enough to avoid getting shot while lying down. Glad to see you sometimes pay attention."

He nodded and didn't mention that he'd just taken the room they gave him.

She pulled the curtains shut then rummaged in her backpack. She set a small jar on the table.

"Roll up your pants and let me take a look at your shins. This ointment should help them heal faster."

He sat in the other chair by the desk and tried to roll up the pant leg but soon found they were too narrowly cut to allow him to roll them to his knees. He tried several times but only got an inch or two above his ankle. Jessica stood watching and folded her arms over her chest.

"Just take the pants off if they won't roll up."

"Ah, okay. Just a sec."

He hurried to the bathroom and shut the door on her surprised expression. He couldn't just strip off his pants in front of her. It felt... weird to be so undressed around her. Never mind how much they'd been through together. He peeled off his pants and hung them over the shower door. Now he felt even more uncomfortable about going out there in just his underwear. He snatched a towel from the wrack and wrapped it around his waist. Better than nothing.

She stared at him, one eyebrow raised, as he opened the door and came out, moving toward the chair. He ignored her bemused expression. Her expression faded as she looked at his legs.

He'd run out of proper bandages and just wrapped toilet paper around his lower legs.

"How the hell did you manage to get shot?" she said and she carefully peeled the paper away from his skin.

"One of the vampires got the gun away from us," he said. "I can't recall exactly how. It all happened so fast. I did manage to kill one of them."

"You're lucky it was a crap shot and didn't hit higher up on your legs and sever the femoral artery," she said. "You would have bled out in minutes."

Some of the paper stuck to his wounds. She had to tug at it to remove it, tearing the skin again and making him hiss in pain. She apologized with every tug but it couldn't be helped. It had to come off. A dull ache settled into his legs by the time she finished. She unscrewed the jar and scooped out some ointment. Her fingers spread it across his skin with a light, gentle touch. His skin tingled and the ache diminished. She sat back on her haunches, wiping her hands on a towel.

"How's that?" she said.

"It feels better," he said. "A little weird."

She smiled. "That's the healing properties. It's some kind of eastern root." She stood up and tossed the towel into the bathroom.

"Now I want you to tell me all about this vampire that mentioned Kobol."

He described visiting the parkette to call her, then the arrival of the man and woman. When he reached the part about pulling the vampire off her, Jessica shook her head. He finished with the unsuccessful stabbing with the branch and the vampire threatening him about Kobol.

"And he said 'you won't stop us?'" Jessica said.

"That's right." He nodded.

She frowned, glancing back at her backpack. Finally she crossed the room to retrieve it. She unzipped the main pocket and rooted around inside. She pulled over several sheets of paper and dropped the backpack to the floor.

"I retrieved these from Frank Brammar's house in Ridgewater City," she said. "Morgan was supposed to pass them along but he didn't. He thought it was a bunch of crap. Frank had a lot of odd ideas about the vampires but I think he might have been on to something here." She spread the papers across the desk.

Sebastian got up and joined her to look at the papers. Scrawled handwriting covered the pages, including strange diagrams of triangles and charts. He recognized a few vampire names: Constantine and Kobol in particular. But other names were listed around them and Sebastian imagined they were probably clan heads as well: Tramplain, Jucael, Xavier, Celine.

Strange, Sebastian didn't notice any other female names listed. He pointed at it.

"Celine," he read aloud. "Do you know who that is?"

"No," Jessica said. "Morgan kept these papers to himself after I gave them to him. I only got a chance to look at them once."

"How did you end up with them?"

A smirk crossed her lips. "I stole them. If Morgan couldn't be bothered with them, I figured they were mine." The smile drained from her face. "Frank spent a lot of time on this. Someone should take it seriously."

"He'd like that," Sebastian said.

Jessica's lips trembled until she pressed them together. She glanced back down at them. She blinked several times.

Sebastian wanted to put his hand on her shoulder, let her know he understood how she felt. It was hard to lose a friend. But just as he started to lift his hand, she pointed at a section of the paper.

"Look at this," she said. "Can you read that word?"

He leaned over the page. "His writing is really bad."

"I know. And he was creative with his spelling sometimes," she said.

"I think it says 'lineage.' At least that's what it looks like, that's a 'g' for sure."

She leaned close. He felt her arm press against him but the only scent he caught from her was a slight trace of shampoo. As with all the In-Between, her scent was impossible for him to smell.

"You're right," she said. "It's lineage. That makes so much sense!"

He caught the tinge of excitement in her voice. "What does it mean?"

"Frank was always talking about tracing the roots of vampirism. He always figured it started somewhere and if we could find out where, maybe we could stop it. These are the clan heads, or most of them that Frank could figure out." She pointed at the names. "One of them has to be the eldest. They either have to be one of the originals or the original themselves if we can figure out who."

"How can we do that?"

"It's going to take some digging," she said. "The In-Between has several archives stashed in different locations around the world. The closest is in the UK, in an old mansion owned by Corbin Remington. He and Frank used to write to each other. I'm sure he'd let us take a look at his files, especially if we showed him Frank's work."

He matched her smile. "Sounds like a good plan. We should head off."

"We should probably let your legs heal up for another day," she said. "We can take off tomorrow night."

"All right," he said, "that sounds..."

Behind her, the window exploded inward. A figure landed on the floor, struggling through the curtains. Sebastian heard the telltale snarl of a vampire.

Jessica reached into her backpack and drew two silver knives. She tossed one to Sebastian. He snatched it out of the air as he ran to flank the vampire. One hand appeared, tearing through the fabric. Jessica darted forward and slashed out. The blade sliced through the vampire's hand. It roared in pain. The curtains billowed as the figure underneath fell backward.

"Mercy," it yelled. "Truce!"

Truce? Sebastian mouthed at Jessica. He'd never heard of a vampire asking for a truce. She shrugged and shook her head.

"Who are you?" she said. "What's your name, who's your clan?"

"I'm Gerard," said the vampire from under the curtain. "My clan is Kobol."

"The Kobol who's coming to make me pay dearly," Sebastian said.

"That was Valentine, he made the threat. He doesn't have the authority to do that. You interrupted his feeding and he was angry."

"If you're not here to kill us, why are you crashing through the window?" Jessica said.

The curtain shuddered and fingers pulled the edges down to reveal a thin face, framed with spiked brown hair that stuck out in all directions.

"I had to," Gerard said. "It was the only way to get here before..."

A thud sounded at the door. The door trembled on its hinges. Something growled outside and slammed into the door again. The wood cracked.

"I think maybe you'd better put on your pants," Jessica said.

CHAPTER SIX

Sebastian retrieved his pants from the bathroom and yanked them on. As he ran back into the bedroom, another bang sounded on the door. The crack at the top widened, extending almost a foot down. Sebastian shoved his feet into his shoes. Jessica shoved the papers into her backpack and swung it onto her shoulders, still holding the knife toward the vampire.

Gerard extracted himself from the curtain and backed away to the hole where the window had been.

"Want to tell us who that is?" Jessica said.

"I don't know exactly," Gerard said. "But they're from Constantine."

"Constantine!" Sebastian said.

Gerard nodded. "He doesn't like you very much."

"We should kill this one and get out of here," Jessica said.

"Wait! I came to help you, to warn you."

"You didn't do a very good job," Jessica said.

"Well, sorry about that."

"If you're here to help us, hold them off while we get out," Sebastian said.

Gerard shrugged. "I don't know if I can do that."

"I guess we'll kill you then," Jessica said. She lifted the knife as she stepped closer.

"Wait! Okay, I'll hold them off." Gerard held up his hands. "Just don't stab me. I hate that."

As he moved toward the door, Sebastian stepped to Jessica's side. "Are you sure this is a good idea?"

"Got a better one?" Her whisper matched his own.

"No."

"Then let's hope it works."

"Head to the back. I think there's another stairwell outside."

She nodded.

He grabbed the cell phones and stuffed them in his pockets. Then as a thought, he yanked on two of the t-shirts. At least he wanted to have something to show for the shopping trip.

Another bang shuddered against the door. Gerard snarled and yanked the door open. A hand slashed at him, soaring above his head. Gerard disappeared into the hallway. Angry yells and snarls sounded. Thuds and pounding reverberated through the walls.

Jessica nodded to the door. Sebastian followed as she crept forward. When they reached the door, she stayed low and he peered above her head. Off to the left, he saw Gerard struggling with two other vampires halfway down the hall.

He touched Jessica's shoulder. She darted out, heading right. Sebastian ran after her. The snarls increased. They'd been spotted!

Gerard cried out. Then Sebastian heard footsteps following, gaining as they pounded after him. Jessica reached the back door and threw it open. He watched her disappear down the stairs.

The footsteps were almost upon him. Sebastian's hand tightened on the knife in his right hand. Making a stand here could give Jessica enough time to escape.

He stepped forward with his left foot and pivoted with his right. His hand slashed with the blade, aiming low. The vampire behind him ducked but the blade caught him across the lower chest, slicing through muscle. Blood sprayed out. It splashed on Sebastian's t-shirt even as he jumped back. The vampire screamed and stumbled. He blocked the progress of the one behind him.

Sebastian turned and ran. His shoulder hit the door, swinging it open. He let himself take one glance back.

A familiar face reared up from behind the fallen vampire, glasses still perched on her nose, her hair still cut in that pixie shape. But this time, her mouth twisted in a snarl.

Alexa...

Sebastian turned and ran down the stairs as fast as his legs could carry him.

He ran past Jessica and headed down the alley.

"Sebastian!" Her whispered voice followed him but he kept going. His heart pounded as if it would burst from his chest. Fear and rage warred inside him. He heard footsteps behind him. He spun, lifting the knife.

Jessica's hand grabbed his wrist.

"Whoa there," she said. "I don't think they're following but we'll head for the main street and get a cab." She stopped. "What is it? You look like you've seen a ghost."

He sucked in a breath. "Alexa." The word exploded out of him. "She was there."

"Dammit," Jessica said. "Come on. Let's get out of here fast."

She grabbed his arm and dragged him toward the main street. She slowed as they reached the front of the alley. Stopping a few feet back, she held up her hand to signal him to wait. As she inched forward, peering out, Sebastian stripped off the top t-shirt and tossed it away. Walking around in a blood splattered t-shirt was not the way to avoid attention. The bottom of his other shirt still had a little blood but it wasn't noticeable. Good.

He glanced back up the alley, his hand tightening on the blade. Nothing yet. Would she follow to finish the job? Even thinking about it set his heart pounding. He hadn't seen her for a year, since that night in the cemetery by Charlie's grave. She'd been so nonchalant, offering to let him drink from her arm, to turn him so they could be together. No part of her was left, he'd realized that then. Just as Jessica said. Every part of Alexa was gone, it was just a vampire with her face.

A hand touched his shoulder. He jumped.

"Taxi," Jessica said in his ear.

He followed her into the backseat and the taxi took off into the night.

Jessica leaned forward to give instructions in French to the driver. They talked back and forth for a few minutes before Jessica handed over a ten euro note. A grin spread across the driver's face. He nodded and hit the gas.

"Where are we going?" Sebastian leaned over to her as she sat back.

"We're going to the ferry at Calais. Don't worry, we won't be anywhere near the In-Between."

"You think they aren't going to be looking for me?" he said.

"Relax," she said. "I know how to avoid them when I want to." Her hand touched his arm. "You okay? I know it's a shock."

He let out a slow breath. "Yeah. It's just weird. I wish she'd really... well..."

"Yes, it's easier when they actually die," she said.

The odd tone of her voice made him look at her. She was staring straight ahead, an almost blank look on her face as if she was lost in thought. A few strands of hair had come loose from her ponytail and hung down on the left side of her face. He wanted to tuck those strands behind her ear, behind the small diamond stud earrings she always wore. She never changed them, never removed them. Not that their lives gave her much chance to dress up and wear different earrings. Maybe they should do something like that, he thought. Get dressed up, go out for dinner somewhere. Be normal people once in a while.

The ache that started in his chest surprised him. He'd thought he'd buried those desires. Guess not.

Jessica grabbed her backpack and pulled it onto her lap. She unzipped the small front pocket. Funny, he'd never seen her open that pocket. He thought she never used it. Instead she pulled out a small plastic photo book. She pushed the backpack off her lap and onto the floor. Her hand trembled holding the photo book. Her fingers whitened where she gripped it.

Her lips pressed tight together then her breath shot out as she seemed to come to a decision. Her head bowed as she opened the book.

"This... this is my brother, Tommy." Her voice was a soft whisper in the car. He barely heard it over the hum of the engine. He bowed his head to match hers and looked at the photo.

The smiling face of a young boy looked out. He was sitting on a seesaw on a playground. Colorful blurs of other children dotted the playground behind him. Sunlight made the paint on the seesaw glow. A wind had sent the boy's brown hair flying. The photo caught it in midflight. The slope of his jaw line and cheeks had the same look as Jessica's, he could see her in the boy's face.

"Where?" Sebastian kept his voice low.

She didn't reply and continued staring at the photo. He thought she hadn't heard him. Should he speak again? He didn't want to intrude but she'd pulled out the photo for a reason. In the year they'd known each other, this was the first time she'd ever shown him anything of her life before the In-Between. Maybe she was regretting it.

"He's gone." Her voice trembled. "We were camping. It was the summer after my dad died. He'd always taken us camping so my mom wanted to keep up the tradition. We had these two tents and I had to share with Tommy. He snored and I hated it. So I took off to have a smoke near the washrooms. It was one of those camp sites where they had washrooms about a fifteen minute walk away. That's why I couldn't hear them when they attacked."

Her voice caught. She stopped for a few moments and he listened to her breathing, taking fast breaths in and out of her mouth. He waited while she got control of herself again.

"Sometimes I wonder if I'd been there but I know that's stupid. They would have killed me too. By the time I got back, they must have been full. That's why they couldn't finish me. That and I screamed so loud I practically woke up the entire park. People came running from all over but it was too late. My mom lived for a full day but Tommy..."

The book shook in her hands. He reached out to steady her grip. Her face lifted to him. He saw tears shimmering in her eyes.

"I'm sorry," he said.

She shook her head. A tear trembled on the bottom of her right eyelid but didn't fall.

"He came to the hospital the next night." Her voice had a dead, dull tone. "He wanted me to come with him. I almost wanted to even though I could tell it wasn't Tommy anymore. It just had his face. I almost gave in and I might have if Frank and Gareth, another In-Between, hadn't shown up. Frank read the newspapers and learned about the attack. It's easy to spot if you know what to look for, he always used to say that. He and Gareth stopped Tommy but said it was up to me if I wanted to finish it." She turned back to the photo and closed her eyes. "Frank held Tommy down while I cut his head off. My mom died two hours later. She never woke up and she never came back."

He put his arm around her. She sat straight for a moment longer and then yielded, leaning against him. He rested his cheek on her head, feeling the softness of her hair. Her head rested in the crook of his shoulder and after a moment he felt her arm snake around him and she clung on. He felt dampness on his t-shirt. His arm tightened around her. After a little while, the dampness dried but he didn't want to let her go. She made no move to pull away and he kept his arm around her, feeling her warmth against him.

They sat like that for the entire ride to the ferry in Calais.

<hr>

As they reached the ferry dock, Jessica pulled away, stuffing the photo book back into the front pocket of her backpack. Her regular business-like expression slipped back down on her face. She handed the driver another ten euro note and he responded as if she'd handed him a thousand. They clambered out of the taxi and waved him away.

They grabbed the first ferry crossing and disembarked in Dover. Jessica snagged a car and by nine they were on the road. Sebastian squinted against the sunlight that pounded at his temples. Every time they made a turn, he almost commented about her driving on the wrong side of the road but always just stopped himself. Funny how even after a year he still wasn't used to people driving on the left side of the road.

He closed his eyes against the offensive sunlight and listened to the hum of the car engine. After a time, the hum stopped. He started, blinking the gumminess out of his eyes. He must have slept but he didn't remember. Jessica was looking at him with her regular bemused expression.

"Ready, sleeping beauty?" she said. "You might want to wipe the dribble from your chin."

He swiped his arm across his mouth as she got out of the car. He followed, shutting the door as he gazed up at the mansion in front of him. The car sat in a circular drive. He glanced around seeing large grounds. The lawns were somewhat patchy, as if they had been ignored for a time. Along the front of the house, an empty garden shot lengths of vines that hung lethargic and half withered on the red brick. As he looked closer, he noticed the late afternoon sun twinkling oddly off one of the upstairs windows.

"Jessica," he said.

She'd taken several steps toward the front door but his tone made her stop. She looked back at him. "What?"

He pointed up to the window. Her gaze followed. A frown darkened her face.

"Weapons," she whispered to him. They grabbed the silver knifes and held them down by their legs as they moved to the front door. He flanked it to the left as she moved to the right. Her hand tightened on the door knob. She nodded to him. He nodded back. She twisted the door knob and shoved the door open.

It banged against the wall and began to rebound. Jessica jumped in, crouching low, knife at ready. Sebastian followed, flanking her across the right, holding his knife ready.

The foul stench of death hit them as soon as they crossed the threshold. The bodies of two men lay in the center of a large foyer. Dead for some time from the smell of them.

Jessica shut the door and crossed to the bodies. The worry lines deepened on her forehead. She signalled to Sebastian for the stairs. He followed as she moved toward the sweeping staircase that curved along the wall and up to a second floor. All through the house, they found signs of battle, shattered windows, overturned furniture and yet more bodies, with throats torn out, blood long soaked into rugs or dried on the walls. One was even missing a head.

They made their way down the back staircase and went outside at the back of the house. Both of them sucked in fresh air, filling their lungs.

Sebastian coughed, trying to get the smell out of his nostrils. He might have to burn his clothes to get rid of the stench.

"He's not here," Jessica said. It was the first thing either of them had said since they reached the house.

"None of those men were Remington?" Sebastian said.

She shook her head. "Corbin is a short fat man with cropped blond hair. All those people were In-Between."

Sebastian shivered. "Vampires."

"Looking for Corbin or for what Corbin knew. There's something going on. This is the most blatant attack I've ever seen. And with that raid..." She kicked at a piece of gravel and sent it spinning across the yellow grass. "I don't know. Something big is brewing but I don't know what it is."

"I think it's time we found out," he said.

She barked out a laugh. "From where? Do you think any In-Between are going to answer our questions? Not after that raid."

"Maybe there's something here then, something the vampires missed."

"And if there isn't?"

He took a breath and let it out slow. "Then maybe we need to try something radical. Like talking to the vampires."

Her mouth dropped open. "Are you kidding me?"

"I'm not the one who sent a vampire to warn us about Constantine sending a couple of his vampires after us. Maybe what ever is going on is worrisome to some of those vampires, or at least to Kobol. Maybe he'll talk to us."

"That's crazy," she said.

"Does that mean you won't even consider it?"

She sighed. "It means we leave it for a last resort. Like very last. Like I've lost my mind resort. For now, let's check the house. I know Corbin had a lot of hidden cubby holes."

"Can we leave some windows open?" he said. "It's hard to breathe in there."

"Breathe through your mouth," she said. "It's easier."

She lied, but he followed her back in.

In the end they opened all the windows but it still didn't make much difference. Jessica found some handkerchiefs in an upstairs closet and they tied them around their noses and mouths. It helped a little, but not much. He felt like he could taste the decay and it was all he could do not to vomit.

They searched through the house, top to bottom. Most of the hidden cubby holes were upstairs or in the library and office on the main floor. No matter how he tried to figure out how she found them, he couldn't do it and had to follow her from room to room. Jessica would stand in the doorway, then move to a section of the wall and tap. Sometimes she would tap on the floor. Invariably after a few minutes of this tapping, she would peel up a section of the floor, or look behind a picture or piece of furniture, and a section of the floor or wall would pop free. Sebastian couldn't figure out how she did it; all the tapping sounded the same to him, even with his enhanced hearing.

Unfortunately, each cubby hole turned up empty. Jessica's expression became grimmer with each failure until she openly scowled. Finally with the last one in the office, on the floor behind the desk, she banged her fist on the wall.

"Dammit, empty again."

"What now?" Sebastian said.

"I don't know. I have to think."

"Can we think outside?" he said. "It's kind of smelly in here."

She stood up, brushing dust from her pants. "Well, that is one thing we can take care of."

"Oh?" he said.

Then he found out he wasn't so thrilled with her idea.

She dragged him to a large back shed where they found several shovels. She picked a spot out back and began digging. Sebastian stood holding his shovel.

"Come on, help me," she said. "You're strong. It won't take so much time."

"And why are we burying them? Why don't we call the police?"

"You really think the police can do anything except get themselves killed or turned?" she said. "Besides, you're the one who keeps complaining about the smell."

"Good point." He dug the shovel into the ground.

Heaving the dirt out of a hole was mind-numbing work but he found he welcomed it. It was a simple, basic task that didn't involve ambiguity or confusion. Dig a hole. Make it deep enough and wide enough for the six bodies in the house. When she signalled him to stop, he was surprised at how close the sun was to the horizon. They'd been digging for some time.

They retied the handkerchiefs around their faces and retrieved the bodies from the house. Using linens from the closet, they wrapped them up and dragged them out to the hole. They dumped each body into the hole. Fortunately, Remington didn't have any neighbors for miles. It was probably why the bodies hadn't been discovered yet either.

After dumping the last body, Jessica made one final circuit through the house and then returned to help Sebastian fill in the hole. The filling in took much less time than the digging and soon they were patting down the last of the dirt. Sebastian moped his forehead with his t-shirt.

"I could use a drink," Jessica said. "You?"

"Only if you pour generously," he said.

They dumped the shovels back in the shed and returned to the house. Without the bodies, the smell had diminished but still lingered. They left all the windows open.

Jessica retrieved glasses from the kitchen but found no alcohol, nor did they find any in the living room on the main floor.

"Was Corbin a teetotaller?" Sebastian said.

"Absolutely not," Jessica said. "He and Frank used to argue over scotch."

"Let's try his office."

Although no one had died in this room, the rug in the office seemed to hold the stench of death, even with the window wide open.

Sebastian set his glass down on the desk, pushing aside a mess of papers, most shredded beyond any help. He lifted the edge of the rug.

"Let's dump this outside," he said. "It's pretty rank."

Jessica frowned but nodded. "Okay." She set her glass down and picked up the other end. They rolled the large rug back over the wood floor and exposed a large recessed trap door.

They both stopped and looked at each other. Jessica held a finger to her lips and then slipped out of the room. She returned holding two knives. She handed one across to Sebastian then held up three fingers. He nodded. She mouthed the words: one, two, three!

She grabbed the handle and yanked the door up. Sebastian prepared to strike. Nothing. Stale air drifted out, carrying the stench of blood and sickness. He blinked as he stared down in the blackness. Each blink brought everything into sharper relief. He saw a ladder leading down to a dirt floor. From the angle of the entrance, he couldn't see much farther into any room below.

"I'm going down," he said.

"Watch yourself," she said.

Keeping his knife in hand, he climbed down, checking both sides after each step. Nothing came at him. As he moved, the smell of sickness strengthened. Someone was injured or ill down here. Had they hidden from the vampires down here?

He reached the bottom and crouched, surveying the room. Large brown boxes lined one wall. Another wall contained various jarred and condensed food. Across from the ladder, a single cot sat against the wall and a man lay half on it, his legs hanging off as if he'd just managed to make it to the cot and collapsed before he could properly lay down.

The sick smell definitely came from him but Sebastian wasn't taking any chances. He crept forward, staying low, sweeping his gaze around the room as he moved toward the figure. Every sense told him there was no one else in the room. As he reached the man, he finally allowed himself to accept that. He touched the man's clammy shoulder and pulled him over onto his back. A gurgling breath issued from his mouth. Thinning blond hair was matted to his squarish head. A large belly moved little, betraying his shallow breathing.

"Jessica!" Sebastian said.

She jumped down and landed in a crouch.

"I think we found your friend Corbin."

"Dammit." She hurried over and made a quick check on him. A bad gash across his upper arm and shoulder looked like it might be infected. The diseased smell was strongest from there.

"We have to get him out of here," she said.

"We're going to have to rig something. We can't carry him."

In the end, they used a bedsheet tied into a large enclosed hammock shape. They lay Corbin into it and ran rope up the ladder toward the window. Jessica brought the car around and they fastened the rope to the trailer jack at the back of the car.

"Drive really slow," Jessica instructed. "I'll be guiding him upward. Are you sure you can hear me?"

"I can hear you," he said. With all the windows open, he could almost hear her breathing and her heart beat if he concentrated enough.

She didn't need to know how often he'd listened for both.

He started the car, listening to her breathe even over the growl of the engine. He allowed the car to inch forward, then paused to listen more, another few inches, then a pause, again another few inches. Her voice called for him to stop only three minutes into it.

He set the parking brake and jumped out of the car. When he ran into the office, Jessica had Corbin stretched out on the floor. She unwrapped the bedsheet.

"Get him some water," she said.

Sebastian hurried to comply. On the way, he grabbed some towels and ointment from the downstairs bathroom. She used one of the smaller towels to wet the man's lips and dripped water into his mouth. After a moment, he started to automatically swallow. Jessica lifted his head into her lap and continued giving him more water. After a few minutes, his eyes fluttered. His large body shuddered. Delicate fingered hands jerked. His mouth sucked at the towel. Jessica lifted the glass to his lips, tilting it a little to allow more water to flow into his mouth. He swallowed although most dribbled down his chin. Finally the eyes opened, bloodshot and feverish. Jessica pulled the glass away.

"Momma..." His voice came out in a croak.

"He's delirious," Sebastian said. "It's the infection. Let's get him onto the couch."

As they moved him, he fell back into unconsciousness. Sebastian noticed Jessica chewing the inside of her cheek. It was bothering her more than she let on.

"Get me some hot, salt water and all the towels you can find," he said. "We have to clean out the wound."

She hurried to comply.

Cleaning the wound took up almost all the towels. The amount of blood and pus surprised him but when he reached regular tissue, he could tell from the scent of it that although it still held infection, it wasn't as bad as it looked. The man would still need antibiotics. Sebastian applied as much ointment as possible and gave it a light covering with the bandages.

He and Jessica gathered up the towels and carried them to the washing machine. He set it to extra hot and dumped in extra soap. He wanted those towels as sterilized as possible.

They spent the night watching over Corbin, checking the bandages, cleaning the wound, and adding ointment as needed. Around eleven his fever spiked and he began mumbling, waving his hands around. Sebastian thought Jessica was going to chew a hole through the side of her cheek. He finally sent her upstairs to rest, telling her they should take shifts and he would call her in a few hours. He had to almost push her physically up the stairs and stand at the bottom to make sure she walked all the way up.

At midnight, he closed most of the downstairs windows, including the one in the office. Corbin rested quietly. From what Sebastian could tell, the fever seemed to have broken. The man slept deeper now and no longer soaked the towel that Sebastian used to wipe his forehead. By the time the sun rose, Corbin's breath came easier. The wound smelled only of ointment.

A flurry of steps sounded from the stairs. Sebastian moved to the door to intercept her but Jessica pushed her way in.

"What happened to the shifts? Two hours," she snapped. "You were supposed to wake me in two hours. This is damn well longer than two hours!"

"You needed the rest," he said.

She slapped his shoulder. "You aren't my mother. I don't need you deciding what's best for me. How dare you just assume?"

Her voice got louder. He tried to pull her out of the room but she twisted away from him. Her face darkened in anger.

"Just what the hell..."

"Jessica?" A weak voice sounded from the couch. "Is that you?"

CHAPTER SEVEN

Jessica spun away from Sebastian and hurried across the room. She crouched in front of the man lying on the sofa. His hand fluttered up and she captured it in both of hers.

"Corbin!"

A weak smile spread across his pale face. "It's so good to see you, my dear. I never thought I would do so again."

"What happened in here? We found bodies of In-Between."

A spasm of anguish crossed the large man's face. "They were trying to protect me. I thought we had time but..." He stopped. Alarm registered as he caught sight of Sebastian. Jessica caught his gaze and glanced over her shoulder.

"It's okay, Corbin, he's with me. He's my friend Sebastian, another In-Between."

The man visibly relaxed but fatigue made his eyes droop. Jessica patted his hand and rested it on his chest.

"You rest some more and we'll talk later," she said. "Okay?"

The man nodded. His eyes closed even before he finished. His breath deepened into sleep.

Jessica stood up and marched across the room to Sebastian. She grabbed his arm and propelled him through the door and then up the stairs. Her grip didn't loosen as she followed him. She let him go only when they reached the second floor and she shoved him into a small bedroom. He stumbled and caught himself on the side of the bed. He waited as she advanced on him, wondering if she was going to punch him. Instead, she rested her hand against his cheek.

"Thanks for looking after him and letting me rest." He started to smile but her hand slapped his cheek.

"Ow," he said.

"It's not your job to only look after me, it's our job to make sure we're both taken care of. That means splitting any watch duty. Now I'm rested and you're not. If we needed to move fast, you'd be a drag on us. There's a reason for spelling each other. Get it?"

"Yes," he said. "I get it."

"Don't do it again." Her hand slapped his cheek again, making it sting.

"Hey!"

Her stern expression held for a moment longer then he saw her lips curl at the edges. She was enjoying putting him in his place! Without thinking, he grabbed her waist, yanking her closer. Her body bumped against him. Her face stopped an inch apart from his. He couldn't smell her at all, but he heard the thud of her heart beat as it sped up.

Almost as much as his sped up.

Her lips parted the tiniest amount. Her chin lifted a centimeter. He barely had to lean forward to kiss her.

Her lips felt softer than he'd imagined (and he'd imagined it often when no one else was around). A moment later, he felt her arms around him. Her body molded against him, her breasts pressed against his chest. One of her hands clenched his buttocks, pulling him closer to her. He felt himself harden. Her kiss became more urgent.

He pulled her down to the bed, where he didn't rest for quite some time.

When he awoke the quality of light behind the curtain had shifted to late afternoon. He was alone in the bed. His hand moved along the mattress, trying to find the indentation where her body had rested beside him but he couldn't tell. She left no scent for him to smell except the briefest trace of shampoo. Without that, he would have thought he'd imagined the whole thing, the feel of her soft skin, her lips, her breasts, how her legs opened to him.

Enough. He didn't need to get himself going again. That would be way too easy and they were not exactly in a situation to take advantage of it.

He swung his legs out of the bed and padded naked across the room. He opened the door, listening. Nothing. He swung the door wider and crossed to the bathroom. Inside, he locked the door and used the toilet before taking a fast shower.

He closed his eyes as the water ran over his skin. He'd spent so much time mourning Alexa, mourning his old life. How much longer could he spend doing that? Forever? What was the good of that? And yet even as he'd mourned, he'd noticed Jessica always there, always supporting him, taking his side when the others suspected him because he reacted so much stronger to light, sensed vampires so much more keenly. They thought of him as a freak among freaks but she'd never treated him that way. How many times over the past year had he lay at night thinking about her? More times than he'd admitted to himself. And after this last disastrous raid, his only thought had been to make sure she was okay.

He'd loved Alexa with the puppy dog infatuation of first love and maybe a part of him would always love her, would always mourn for what would never be, because now she was a symbol of his old life, of how it might have been if he'd not walked into those woods late one Thursday night. He'd have finished college, maybe they would have connected at some point. He would have got a job, got married, maybe a kid or two.

A normal life.

But the In-Between don't have normal lives. They had lives of shadow and death. He'd never have that life with Alexa.

Instead he had Jessica. Even if only for a few hours. That could be enough, if it had to be.

Although he knew he wanted more.

He dressed, rubbing the water from his hair and leaving it drying in disarray as he headed downstairs. The smell of food soon overpowered the lingering scent of decay. He found Jessica in the kitchen. Corbin Remington sat in a chair next to the wall. He leaned on both the wall and the table in front of him. He jerked a little as Sebastian walked in. Sebastian caught a whiff of fear emanating off the man. He was still a little skittish.

Sebastian didn't blame him one bit.

"I'm making fried potatoes and eggs," Jessica said. "Can you set the table?" She nodded at the stack of plates on the counter.

"Sure." He picked up the plates and carried them to the table. By the time he finished setting them out with cutlery, napkins and glasses, Jessica carried over the frying pan with the eggs. She scooped two out onto each plate then she retrieved a second pan and doled out the pan fried potatoes. After dumping the pans in the sink and running water over them, she returned to her place at the table. They all began to eat.

"How did you sleep?" she said.

He chewed and swallowed a piece of egg before replying. "Fine. How are you feeling, sir?"

Corbin seemed to have trouble lifting the fork with his right hand. He switched to his left. "Alive. Which I wouldn't be if not for you both."

"I want to get you out of here as soon as possible," Jessica said. "It's not safe for you here by yourself. Maybe you should go to Madame Prommare or Lester Dickson."

"I'm not sure how safe they'd be," Corbin said.

"Can you tell us what happened?" Sebastian said. Jessica shot him a warning look. He clamped his mouth shut. Too late to call the words back.

"Let him eat," Jessica said. "I want you to finish everything. You need your strength."

Corbin moved the fork around his plate. "I will. I was working on a translation of a text I'd received from the In-Between. An old book, purported to be one of the oldest books by a vampire, written on human flesh. All sorts of wild rumors surround it. It's supposed to hold great magic. It foretells the end of the world and who will bring it."

"Does it happen to end on December 21st?" Sebastian said.

"Sebastian!" Jessica's eyes flashed a warning.

Corbin snorted a laugh. "I had the same reaction. Sounded like a bunch of mumbo jumbo to me. But when they brought it to me..." He shook his head. "I can only say I felt something strange in the presence of that book. Evil and something else."

"Did you get far in the translation?" Jessica said.

He shook his head. "Barely started it but I can tell you one thing. The pages were made from human flesh."

Sebastian shuddered.

"The vampires took it back," Jessica said.

"No. I suspected they were coming and I moved it before they got here. The In-Between wanted me to give it to them, sent their troops to guard me and the book but you saw the success of that mission."

"Where's the book now?" Sebastian said.

Corbin glanced up at him. Sebastian could smell the uncertainty floating over an undercurrent of fear.

"It's safe for now."

"If you feel up to it later, I have some notes I'd like you to take a look at," Jessica said. "I need your opinion on what they mean."

"Notes? From where?"

Jessica looked down at her plate. "They were Frank's."

"Oh. Yes, I'll look at them. He'd want me to help you."

They finished the rest of the meal in silence.

After, Sebastian helped Jessica stack the dishes in the sink. He tried to catch her eye, to gauge her mood but she kept her gaze fixed on the plates. Even her heart beat at a steady rhythm. She turned to take Corbin his cup of tea.

"Thank you, my dear," he said as she set the cup in front of him. He took a sip and sighed. He even seemed to sit a little straighter, as if the tea held healing powers that no food or rest could match.

"That's better. More civilized. It always feels like things will be all right when you've got a cup of tea." A melancholy smile crossed his face. "Complete lie but a comforting one. Let me see Frank's notes now, Jessica. You, boy, sit here." He pointed at the chair across from him.

Sebastian slid onto the chair as Jessica left to retrieve the notes from her backpack upstairs. Corbin took another sip of tea and peered across the table at Sebastian.

"I thought you were a vampire when I first saw you," Corbin said. "You've got the look."

Sebastian blinked in surprise. "The look?"

"Mmm, the paleness, the gliding movements, even that look in the eyes, watchful. Must have been close with you."

"I... I don't know," Sebastian said. "I don't remember it all that well."

"How did you get away?"

"I didn't. Bianca, the vampire who tried to turn me, got interrupted before she could finish."

Corbin frowned. "Bianca? I don't recall a clan head with that name."

"She wasn't a clan head. She was turning me on her own."

Corbin almost choked on his tea. He set the cup down and coughed into his fist. Sebastian started to stand to hurry over to him but Corbin waved him back down. The coughing subsided, leaving the man's face blotchy. He picked up the tea again and took a small sip.

"That explains a lot," he said. "She got you almost all the way. It's a surprise you didn't die, boy." His fingers fiddled on the cup. "Might have been a blessing."

Sebastian thought of his best friend Charlie, now dead, and Alexa, now turned. "It might have been. Nothing I can do about it now."

"No, I suppose there isn't. Funny how that's the way of many things in life."

Jessica returned with the papers. Corbin moved his tea to the side and spread the papers along the table in front of him. His delicate fingers moved along the pages almost as if he was reading them with his eyes and his fingers. A line appeared in his forehead and deepened as he read. By the time he finished, a frown had turned down his lips and the line in his forehead had been joined by others. He flipped back to the first page and started reading again. Sebastian looked over at Jessica, trying to catch her eye but she was watching Corbin with intense concentration.

Finally he finished reading the pages a second time. He leaned back from them and took a sip from his tea. That made him frown even more.

"Cold," he said.

"I can warm it up." Sebastian got up from the table, reaching for the cup.

"No, sit down. We need to discuss this." He tapped the pages.

"Important?" Jessica said.

"Very. I wish I'd had these when I had the book. Some of the phrasing, it might have helped. And Frank's theories about the clan heads. Yes, it would have made it much easier to translate. I have to wonder if Frank somehow got his hands on a copy of this book or had seen it at some point."

"Did you tell him about Kobol?" Sebastian said.

Corbin's eye brows raised. "Kobol? What about him?"

Sebastian hesitated.

Jessica spread her hands. "Go ahead, you started it. Tell him." From the thinning of her lips, he could tell she wasn't pleased that he mentioned it but it was too late to pull it back now.

"He sent one of his men to us in Rouen, to warn us that Constantine had sent some of his people after us."

Corbin's mouth dropped open. "Kobol sent someone to warn you? A vampire?"

"Yes."

"Kobol, the vampire, a clan head?"

"Yes," Sebastian said.

Corbin leaned back in his chair, clearly dumbfounded. "I've never heard of such a thing. A vampire warning a human about another vampire." He shook his head in wonder.

"I was thinking," Sebastian said. He hesitated. Even in his own head the thought sounded crazy. But now he had their attention. Even Jessica had turned to look at him and she hadn't looked at him directly since he'd come down stairs.

"Yes?" Corbin said.

"I was thinking maybe we should contact Kobol."

"That's crazy!" Jessica said. "No way! Corbin, tell him."

"That's an interesting thought," the old man said.

Jessica spun on him. "What?"

"I said it's an interesting thought. There's definitely something going on, something at the highest levels. Getting information from Kobol may be something to consider but not just yet." He frowned, his hand fiddling with the tea cup. "I need to see that book again. With Frank's notes, I think I could translate it and we need to know what's in it."

"You said the book was safe," Sebastian said. "Can you get it back?"

"It is safe, but it was a one way trip," Corbin said.

"What do you mean?" Jessica said.

""I can't recall it," Corbin said. "It has to be retrieved in person. I don't think I'm in any shape to travel."

"We can get it for you," Sebastian said. He glanced over at Jessica.

She nodded. "But only if you go somewhere safe."

"You know that's a misnomer," Corbin said. "But I can find somewhere safer."

"Good," Jessica said. "Now tell us where you sent the book."

"It's not so much where as who," the old man said.

Even before he started to tell them more, his eyelids drooped and his body listed to the side. That was enough for Jessica to stop him and insist he get some rest. They could make do for another night here and then they would move somewhere else. No one would expect them to be here so they should be safe.

Sebastian and Jessica helped Corbin up the stairs and put him in the nearest bedroom, a small room opposite the one Sebastian had claimed. The man was asleep before they shut the door on him.

Jessica turned and moved down the stairs. Sebastian had to hurry and only caught up to her at the bottom as she headed toward the kitchen at the back of the house.

"Jessica..."

"What were you thinking saying we should talk to Kobol?" she said. "Are you nuts?"

That hadn't been what he'd wanted to talk about. "He did send someone to warn us about Constantine's people."

"Did it ever occur to you that maybe it was so he could have us to himself?"

"Then why didn't his people come to get us? They obviously knew where we were."

She shook her head. "We're taking Corbin somewhere safe tomorrow, once he's had another night's rest."

"And then?"

"Then we'll figure out our next move." She didn't look at him.

"That's not what I mean."

"I know what you mean," she said. "What do you want me to say? We should get a little house with a white picket fence? That's not our lives. You have to take what you can get and be grateful for it. I can't be Alexa for you."

She turned away toward the sink and started running the water.

"I didn't think you were," he said.

The dishes clattered under her hands as she started washing them.

"Jessica..."

"I don't know what you want from me." Her hand came down on the counter, holding a plate. It shattered, spending shards of pottery skittering across the counter. A piece nicked her index finger. Blood welled up on the end.

"Dammit," she said.

"Here." He took her hand and held it under the water to wash it out. Then he grabbed a towel and wrapped it around her hand, getting her to hold it up in the air. Her hand trembled in his and he didn't think it was from holding it up.

She wouldn't look at him. He touched her chin and tilted her face up.

"I can't," she said.

He could hear the unspoken words in her tone: *be her*. He brushed away a strand of stray hair the way he had always imagined doing it, tucking it behind her ear.

"I don't want you to be her," he said. "I want you to be you because you're the only one since this whole thing started that hasn't acted as if I'm crazy or a freak. Even Corbin said he thought I was a vampire at first and I know the In-Between don't trust me. You're the only one who's stood by me without question. Do you think I didn't notice?"

Moisture shimmered in her eyes. She yielded as he pulled her closer to him. Her mouth opened when he kissed her and her tongue met his. Her free arm curled around his neck. His hand pressed at the small of her back, holding her against him.

The sound of shattering glass broke the spell. It came from the front of the house. Jessica jumped away from him, racing out the door. Sebastian ran to follow, stopping to grab several knives from the cutting board first.

Glass from the shattered window on the door covered the floor. The door had been unlocked and flung open. Footsteps already sounded upstairs. Jessica leapt up the stairs two at a time. Sebastian outpaced her, his long legs eating up the stairs three at a time.

He reached the top and saw the door to Corbin's room open. He ran inside. Corbin lay on the bed, one hand battering at a figure bent over him. Sebastian lunged forward, swinging with one of the knives. It sank into the figure's back right up to the hilt.

With a snarl, the vampire straightened. It backhanded Sebastian across the face, sending him spinning across the room. He grabbed onto a dresser to arrest his fall. Fangs glinted in the creature's mouth. Blood smeared its chin and cheeks. It growled at Sebastian and took a step forward, raising a clawed hand to finish the job.

Jessica appeared in the doorway. She unsnapped something from her belt and flung it forward. It sliced across the vampire's ear and embedded itself into the wall. The vampire screamed, grabbing the side of its head as blood spurted. The ear flopped onto the area rug.

The vampire turned on Jessica. She lifted another silver Shuriken. With a hiss, the vampire spun away and ran at the window. It crashed through, sending glass spraying out onto the dying lawn below.

Sebastian ran to the bed. Corbin's neck pulsed blood. Sebastian pressed his hand against the wound, trying to staunch the flow.

"Get some bandages," he shouted to Jessica. She ran from the room.

Corbin's eyes opened. One pupil looked dilated, the other was too large. His skin had a pasty, white glue look to it.

"Hang on, Corbin," Sebastian said. "Just hang on. We'll take care of you."

The old man's mouth moved. Beneath his hand, Sebastian felt Corbin's heart beat slow. His blood was already taking on the sour smell of impending death. Sebastian pressed harder, as if pressure could stop the man's life from slipping away.

Please...

Corbin's mouth movements became more frantic. Finally Sebastian put his ear to the man's mouth. His grip on the old man's neck loosened. He couldn't keep up the same pressure in this position but Corbin seemed to have something to say.

"Book." His voice came in a breathy gasp. "Find. Chat Stan. Book."

He seemed to be repeating himself. Sebastian pulled his head away, tightening his grip on Corbin's neck again to try to stop the bleeding.

"It's okay, Corbin, we'll find the book and you'll translate it for us. It'll be okay."

Corbin's eyelids fluttered. His mouth stopped moving.

Jessica ran in, carrying towels and wads of bandages. She unrolled one and pressed one against Sebastian's fingers. He released, allowing her hands to take his place. But Corbin's eyes already had the far away look in them that Sebastian had now seen too many times. He grabbed onto Jessica's wrist.

"Don't," he said.

"But Corbin..." She looked at Sebastian in confusion. Then she looked down at the old man. "Corbin."

Her hand relaxed in Sebastian's and she allowed him to pull her away. He grabbed towels, handed one to her and wiped his hands with another. Her hands moved mechanically. More footsteps sounded from downstairs. He could see it jolt her out of grief. She sucked in a breath and he could hear her heartbeat quicken.

She jerked her head at the door. He gave a nod. They peered through the doorway. Nothing yet, but the house was big with multiple entrances and windows. The vampires could come at them from any angle.

Jessica darted into the hallway, running in a crouch to the next doorway on this side. Her hand reached in and pulled out her backpack. She yanked out two silver knives and passed one to Sebastian. He took it as she slipped the backpack on her shoulders.

He crooked his finger at her. She stepped to his side, moving her head closer.

"Papers, kitchen." He barely breathed the words but she gave a nod. They had to retrieve the papers before they could take off.

She pointed to the back. They headed that way, moving in a fast crouch, skirting the walls and jumped across the doorways. One minute after they began running, thundering steps sounded on the front stairs. Sebastian risked one glance back. Two large vampires appeared, heading toward them.

So much for stealth.

"Go!" Sebastian yelled.

Jessica surged forward. Even with her shorter legs, she was a faster sprinter than Sebastian. She sailed down the back stairs. Sebastian lagged behind. As he passed one open door, he grabbed a chair from just inside and sent it spinning down the hallway. Vampire one crashed into it but the second vampire vaulted over top, continuing pursuit.

Not so easy to get rid of him.

Sebastian didn't bother with another chair but pushed for speed. He could hear the pounding of the vampire behind him, gaining. He reached the stairs and leapt into the air. He hit the landing and rolled. He felt the scrape of claws on his back as the vampire reached for him. His shoulder hit the kitchen floor and he kept rolling. A whirl of images blurred around him. He gained his feet by the table.

By the entrance to the kitchen, Jessica slashed at a pair of vampires who lunged and snarled at her. They were steadily forcing her back. Half the papers still lay on the table, the rest hung out the open pocket of her backpack. Sebastian grabbed the pages from the table and stuffed them into the pack. Claws dug into his shoulders, pulling him back. He let go of Jessica's pack and drove his arms back. His elbows connected but the claws didn't loosen. Vampire two snarled in his ear. Sebastian pulled the knife from his belt and stabbed backward. Before the knife could connect, the vampire threw him forward, against the wall.

Hitting the wall stunned him but Sebastian managed to keep hold of the knife. He shook his head, trying to clear his swimming vision. Jessica's scream filled his ears. No! He stumbled upward.

The back door burst open. Wood shards sprayed the room. Three more vampires rushed into the room. No way could he and Jessica keep them off. But he wouldn't go down without a fight. He pushed a chair out of the way to meet them head on.

The vampires ignored him. Two launched themselves at the vampire holding Jessica. The third leapt through the doorway, knocking the other two back into the hall. Howling snarls filled the air. Jessica staggered back, holding the backpack in her arms. She caught sight of Sebastian and stumbled toward him. He grabbed her arm, pulling her back around the table. He pushed her down into a crouch against the wall and knocked the table over, using it as a shield. They huddled behind it, listening to the shrieks and snarls of the vampires fighting on the other side. Sounds of glass shattering and furniture breaking filled the air. Finally the cacophony of noise dwindled. Howls and snarls trailed through the house, drifting into the darkness outside.

Footsteps sounded on the other side of the table, crunching over glass fragments. The table jerked and spun away, tossed by a vampire that stood over them. Other vampires crowded the hallway and the back door.

Sebastian tightened his arm around Jessica. She had one hand clenching his leg and the other clutching the backpack. She turned her head away from the vampire toward Sebastian. She winced as if awaiting a blow.

"Get up," the vampire said. "Kobol wants to see you."

Part Two: Flesh

CHAPTER EIGHT

The vampires barely let them stand before they were pushing Sebastian and Jessica out the door. Sebastian saw Jessica's gaze shoot upward as they walked through the front foyer past the stairwell. He knew she was thinking of Corbin's body, left lying in the bedroom to rot until someone found him. He squeezed her hand. A muscle in her jaw jumped.

The vampires pushed them through the open hole where the front door had been. They stumbled over dry grass and gravel toward a line of cars crowding the dark driveway. A vampire stepped ahead of them and opened the back of a van then grabbed Jessica's arm. She tried to jerk away but he held fast and shoved her inside. Sebastian clambered after her. He found her sitting near the side and even in the pitch dark he could see anger tightening her face.

He sat next to her, pressing his leg against hers. He felt her lean into him. He put his arm around her and pressed his face into her hair. A weak trace of her shampoo lingered and he breathed it in, the closest thing he could get to her scent. Her face buried itself against his neck. He felt her lips move.

"Corbin?" Her voice was the barest whisper yet he knew the vampires who piled into the front of the van would hear her.

"Shh," he said. "Them."

He felt her head nod once and she went silent. He knew she wanted to talk, to confirm her friend's death but not with the vampires listening in.

The engine started and the van rocked as it moved. He glanced toward the front and realized they'd blocked all the windows in the van. It wasn't just the night making the inside so dark. They'd effectively prevented him from seeing where they were going.

He listened as hard as he could. The texture of the road changed from gravel to asphalt. They slowed, stopped and turned several times but it soon became impossible for him to tell even what direction they were moving in. He glanced down at Jessica. She had the same intense listening look on her face. When she noticed him watching her, she frowned and shook her head.

She couldn't tell where they were going either.

After what felt like an hour, the van slowed to a stop and the engine cut out. Jessica stiffened beside him. He tightened his arm around her. She squeezed his hand. They listened to the front doors open and slam shut, then footsteps crunched on gravel as the vampires circled to the back of the van. A click sounded and the doors swung open.

"Come on," said the vampire who had first spoken to them an hour ago. He waited a moment then made a motion to get into the van to fetch them.

"We're coming," Sebastian said.

Still holding the backpack, Jessica moved first and Sebastian followed. They jumped down. The vampire jerked his thumb at them, indicating they should circle to the front of the van. They started walking, angling to the right of the van.

Sebastian's feet kicked at the pebbles on the driveway. It seemed to be triple the normal width, then as they turned the corner of the van he realized why. They stood in front of an old cathedral. Long abandoned from the look of it, yet remnants of old scaffolding stretched across the front, speaking to a distant attempt to repair the church. A single spire shot up from the roof and Sebastian realized it was a cross with the arms snapped off. Remnants of stained glass clung to the edges of the window panes, showing dark against the wood boards that shuttered the windows. As they approached the doors, stepping up on crumbling concrete steps, Sebastian smelled the moist scent of decay and rot seeping from the wood and brick of the church. Jessica's noise crinkled, signalling that she smelled it too.

The vampires steered them through the double front doors. Darkness enveloped the inside of the church but with his In-Between sight, Sebastian didn't need any light. He could easily see the abandoned bowls on either side of the door, long empty of any holy water. Most of the pews had been removed, leaving wood shards and nails sticking up from the floor. The few remaining pews lay on their sides in pieces, backs torn off and flung across the empty expanse. A heavy stone altar lay tipped on its side. The walls were empty of any paintings or decor. Above the ruined altar, Sebastian saw the empty mark where the main crucifix would have hung. Someone had scrawled a message across the wall in paint or blood. It was so long dried, Sebastian couldn't even smell it anymore. The message read "Kobol rules."

A vampire pushed them to the right of the altar. A door led out of the main hall of the church. As Sebastian crossed to it, the door opened. Another vampire beckoned them forward, holding the door open. It led to a set of stairs heading down.

Sebastian glanced at Jessica. Her expression was tight and unreadable. They really didn't have much choice.

He headed down first.

The stairs ended in a sub basement. Two large carved wooden doors blocked the way. The vampire that opened the stairwell slipped past them and pushed open the doors. They scraped across the concrete floor, wearing into an old groove. Sebastian stepped forward.

A large, low-ceilinged room spread out before him. Ornate rugs covered the concrete. The walls had been painted so long ago that the paint was now peeling at the top. Large couches sagged against the side walls. A large oak desk spread across the far wall like a squat altar. Two old armchairs sat in front of it, one with a faded, floral pattern, the other a weathered blue.

Around the room, about twenty vampires lounged, sitting on the couches or leaning against the wall. They all coiled with attention at Sebastian and Jessica's appearance.

The vampire at the door pointed them forward. Sebastian took Jessica's hand as they crossed to the chairs. Her fingers gripped his hand in a tight squeeze. As they approached the armchairs, Sebastian noticed a vampire sitting behind the desk in a high back leather chair. His arms rested on the armrests, steepling his fingers in front of his lips. Eyes almost maroon in color stared out from under thick black eyebrows. His head was completely bald, the skin a shining white in the pale light from the weak light bulbs dotting the walls.

Sebastian's feet slowed almost halfway to the armchairs. He felt as if he was being buffeted by a wave of energy. Jessica pressed against his right arm. She made a soft whimpering sound in her throat, so quiet he wasn't sure if he actually heard it or imagined it.

The vampire's eyes narrowed. Sebastian felt another wave of power flood over him. His heart began pounding. Adrenaline coursed into his system, tightening his muscles, raising his anxiety. He felt an almost overwhelming urge to bow down, to kneel, to prostrate himself on the rug, no, to push the rug aside and grovel in the dirt like the maggot he was, beg for acceptance, plead for mercy, scream for the salvation of service...

Sebastian snapped his head to the side, breaking eye contact. He felt Jessica's face pressed against his arm, her tears soaking into his shirt. He put his arm around her shoulders, drawing her close to him. Then he looked back at the vampire sitting behind the desk.

"Did you really bring us here to play some parlor mind control trick?"

Growls and snarls sounded from the vampires around him. Legs swung from armrests onto the floor. Feet stomped on concrete. Hands tightened into fists, as much as claws would allow. Behind the desk, the bald vampire unsteepled his hands and held up his right index finger. The vampires froze. He held up a second finger. The vampires retreated.

Silence filled the room.

The bald vampire lowered his hand, extending his palm toward the two armchairs in front of the desk.

"Please, take a seat." His deep voice rumbled through the room although he spoke just above a whisper.

Sebastian felt the power rumbling even in that phrase. Surrounded by over twenty vampires, they didn't have much choice. He steered Jessica into the blue armchair and he sat in the floral one. Jessica released his hand and sat back. An impassive mask had settled down over her face. She held her backpack on her lap. The grip of her knuckles was the only thing betraying her nerves.

Taking a measured breath, Sebastian turned to face the vampire. Kobol lowered his long fingered hands and rested them on the arms of his chair. A large red jewelled ring glinted on his left hand. He was clean shaven, with a large strong nose above generous lips. His head almost crowned the top of the high backed chair, making Sebastian guess that he was over six feet tall when standing. Even seated in a relaxed posture, he was imposing. Sebastian forced himself not to cower back in the armchair.

"Twice now I have come to your aid," Kobol said. "You should show me some respect."

Sebastian swallowed. "Your aid hasn't been that great. First time we barely got out and the second time our friend was killed."

He felt the vampires shifting around him again, angry murmurs filled the air. Jessica glanced over at him. Her lips pressed tight together.

Kobol's index finger rose again, silencing the vampires. He tilted his head, studying Sebastian. The weight of his stare pressed against Sebastian, almost as if the vampire could peer into his mind, peel away the layers of his thoughts and look deep into the parts even he didn't know he had.

Sebastian's shoulders jerked. He shook his head. Easier to break the spell this time. Kobol's maroon eyes narrowed. He didn't seem to like it.

Too bad, Sebastian thought. There was a lot of stuff going on that he didn't like.

"Are you going to keep trying your mumbo jumbo or are you going to tell us why we're here?" he said.

Kobol leaned back in his chair. The finger wearing the ring tapped on the armrest.

"You are a very interesting In-Between." His voice rumbled through the room. "I believe we can be of assistance to each other."

"Assistance?" Jessica said. "Why would we assist you?"

A smile flittered across Kobol's mouth and vanished as quickly as it came. "Not you. Him. You are of no consequence just a bargaining chip."

Sebastian felt a coldness seep into his chest. "What does that mean?"

"I suspect you know what it means," Kobol said. "You will assist me and I will keep her alive."

Jessica's hands tightened on the backpack. Sebastian knew she probably had a couple of silver knives stashed inside, maybe even some kind of explosive, and while it might take out some of the vampires, it wouldn't take out all of them and there were enough in the room to tear them both apart.

"Threats aren't a very good way to start a negotiation," Sebastian said. "You haven't even told us what you want."

Now the smile spread across Kobol's lips. Sebastian preferred him unsmiling. "Isn't it obvious? I want the book."

"We don't know where it is," Jessica said. "Maybe if your people had been a little faster Corbin might still be alive and he could tell you."

Whatever fear Kobol had instilled in her had burned off. Jessica sat forward in her seat, still clutching the backpack, but this time Sebastian recognized the tenseness of her anger and the flush in her cheeks. Kobol as well seemed to sense the change in her. His attention shifted to her. Sebastian almost felt a wave of energy blast past him. Jessica shuddered. The force of it drove her cowering back into her chair. She pressed her face against the inside of the blue armchair.

"Stop it," Sebastian said.

Kobol ignored him, continuing to focus on Jessica.

Sebastian jumped up in front of Jessica's chair.

It was like stepping in front of a blazing inferno. He felt the power slice into him. His shoulders hunched. His stomach caved in on itself, forcing bile up his throat. He gagged at the burning sensation in his mouth but it helped him focus. He felt fear twisting inside him and while a portion of it was his, he knew a bigger portion was being projected from Kobol. Resisting made him gasp, made him want to run and hide. But that was Kobol's demand. It itched on his skin and picked at his soul until it ignited a flame of anger inside. He'd lost everything because of these damned vampires: his life, his friends, his family, his love, his future, and he wouldn't give them ANYMORE!

A flare of rage seemed to burst out of him. He felt it like a flash of heat, scorching through Kobol's wave of energy. The vampire's attention cracked. His head snapped back against the back of his chair.

The other vampires snarled and jumped forward. Jessica leapt from her chair, yanking a knife out from the backpack. The silver blade glinted in the dim light. Snarls surrounded them.

"Enough!" Kobol's voice sliced through the air. The vampires stayed, still snarling. Kobol drove up from his chair. Like Sebastian expected, he towered over everyone closest to him. Closer to six-six, Sebastian thought.

"What did I say?" the vampire demanded.

The others began to slink away. Low growls sounded as they retreated. The air crackled with Kobol's presence, but without the focus on Sebastian. Still, it made him dizzy after facing so much of the pressure in so short a time. He wanted to stumble back to his chair but he had to make sure Jessica was okay.

He touched her arm, lowering the blade in her hand.

"You okay?" he said.

She nodded. Her face was still pale but he could see her old defiance and strength in her eyes. He felt an overwhelming desire to embrace her, to bury his face in her hair and feel her body against him. His chest seemed to ache with it. Her lips twitched a smile as if she knew what he wanted. Her hand squeezed his arm and released him.

He couldn't embrace her. Not in this place, around these creatures. They already suspected how important she was to him. He wouldn't confirm it for them.

He turned back to his chair and stepped toward it. It took all his concentration not to stumble. He couldn't let Kobol know how much his power affected him. Another blast or two might overwhelm him. He couldn't let the vampire know that.

As he sat, he felt Kobol's gaze on him, measuring, studying. He forced himself to sit up straight. To look steadier and more in control than he felt. Why not? He'd been faking it most of his life.

Kobol sank down into his own seat. "I will not quibble about timing with you. This is not a negotiation. I tell you what I want and you do it. I want the book. You will find it and bring it to me. In exchange, I will give you her life back."

Sebastian opened his mouth but Kobol held up his index finger, interrupting him.

"Think carefully before you speak again, In-Between. I put up with you insolence because I have use for you but I am tiring of it. Your blood may be poison to us, we may not feed off you, but we can tear you both apart in seconds. You can die here."

Now the coldness of fear was all his own. Sebastian swallowed. He glanced at Jessica. She sat ramrod straight in her chair but her shallow breaths betrayed her own fear.

They could die here.

"I don't know where the book is," Sebastian said. "I've never even seen it. I don't know anything about it. I can't get it for you."

"Are you sure you wish to refuse me?" Kobol said.

"I'm not refusing, I'm just telling you I don't know anything about it."

"Then you'll learn and learn quickly." Kobol leaned back in his chair, relaxing, like a tiger reclining on a rock above its prey.

"You will have one week to get the book and bring it to me," the vampire said. "You miss the deadline and you will find her blood coating the ground."

"But..."

"I told you. This is not a negotiation. You will find the book."

"Before Constantine, right?" Jessica said.

Kobol started. His head jerked toward her and he glared at her.

"He's looking for it too, isn't he? That's what you're afraid of, that he'll find it first." Her head tilted. "And he's got a head start, doesn't he?"

"Maybe I should be sending you after the book and keep him as incentive," Kobol said. "Too bad you aren't as strong as he is. You're certainly more clever but he will have to do without your cleverness."

"You really think he can?" Jessica said. "You're expecting a lot. He's only been an In-Between for a year. He doesn't know everything. He won't be able to find your book in a week. Not alone."

One dark eyebrow lifted. "And what is your suggestion?"

"We get it for you," she said.

Kobol snorted a laugh. "And you would do this why?"

"I want Constantine's head on a plate," she said. "He's killed people I care about."

Now his laugh cut across the room. "And that's incentive enough for you to help me? I don't think so."

"You don't know me." Jessica's quiet voice interrupted his laughter. "That's not my only price."

Sebastian stared at Jessica. Her entire body sat rigid, focused forward on Kobol. The hard coldness in her voice sent a chill through Sebastian. He'd never seen her like this, never heard her voice so devoid of emotion.

"Name your price," Kobol said.

"I want one specific vampire who attacked a campground six years ago. I give you the details, you give him or her to me. You get the book. Full exchange."

Kobol's ring finger tapped on the armrest. His maroon eyes studied her. Jessica sat unmoving. Sebastian wished he could smell her, wished he could tell if she was faking it or not. Could she really be that good an actress or was she really willing to bargain away the book for a chance to get revenge for her brother? After six years, would that still be so important to her?

Was it still important to him to want to get Constantine because of Alexa?

He had no right to judge Jessica but that didn't stop the fear from twisting inside his gut.

Kobol sat unmoving. The two of them were so still it made Sebastian want to fidget. His hands curled into fists on his lap. He squeezed them together, feeling his nails bite into the palms of his hands. Still neither Jessica or Kobol moved or made a sound. Kobol wasn't blasting his energy at her, they just stared.

Then Kobol gave a single nod. "Agreed. But you will be accompanied by one of my lieutenants to ensure your cooperation. He is tied to me and I will know immediately if you kill him. If you do there will nowhere on this planet you can hide from me. Are we clear?"

"Yes," said Jessica.

Kobol raised his hand. From behind him, a thin young man stepped forward, gliding in that perfect vampire way. Straight blond hair parted in waves off his narrow face. Pale blue eyes stared out with an impassive, bored expression. He looked like he could pass for fourteen if he didn't carried himself with the surety of an adult.

"This is Leon and he will go with you. You have one week. If you don't find it in one week, Leon will kill you. If you manage to kill him first, I will hunt you down."

"And if we succeed," Jessica said.

"I will give you what you ask for," Kobol said. "And your lives."

He made a dismissive gesture with his hand. Several vampires stepped forward, flanking them on both sides. Leon moved past them.

"Come." His voice sounded musical, speaking the word with an odd cadence. Exactly how old was he, Sebastian wondered.

Clutching the backpack, Jessica stood up and followed the vampire, with Sebastian bringing up the rear. He led them back up the stairs into the ruined church. They shed their followers as they went until they stood outside on the gravel driveway, just the three of them.

"So," Leon said. "Where will we be searching first?"

CHAPTER NINE

Good question, Sebastian thought, then he noticed Jessica looking at him too. Why were they looking at him? He didn't know where to find the book.

"You talked to Corbin when he died," Jessica said.

Sebastian grabbed her arm. "Excuse us," he said to Leon. He started pulling her away. Leon began following then tilted his head after a few steps and stopped. He folded his hands behind his back and waited.

Sebastian dragged Jessica to the end of the driveway before releasing her arm. She yanked it out of his grip and rubbed it.

"Was that necessary?" she said.

"Necessary? You made a deal with a vampire."

"I didn't have much choice. You weren't going to find anything in a week without me. And don't bother looking at him. Of course, he's listening to us."

Sure enough when Sebastian glanced back again, Leon flashed a grin. It looked humorless and odd on his face, like he hadn't smiled in decades.

Sebastian turned to face Jessica. Using the non verbal codes, she'd tried to teach him, he signalled, *We can't turn the book over. Don't know what's in it.*

"Not much choice," she said out loud.

At least she didn't sound happy about it, he thought. Her lips had thinned and the stress crease deepened in her forehead. She lifted two fingers, rubbing her nose and sweeping them across her cheek.

Deal with book later, she'd signalled.

He frowned but tilted his head down. What else could he do?

She stepped around him and returned to Leon.

"I have one more stipulation I forgot to mention," she said.

"What's that?"

"I want to return to Corbin's house and bury him."

The vampire frowned. That expression looked more natural on him, Sebastian thought.

"That's too dangerous," Leon said. "I can't allow it."

Jessica slipped the backpack onto her shoulder and folded her arms across her chest. "We're going whether you allow it or not."

Leon's pale eyes narrowed. He took a step closer to Jessica. No longer did he look like a frail fourteen year old, his slim lethal pose made him look like a cobra about to strike.

"You will do as I say."

Even from a step behind Jessica, Sebastian could smell the sour stench of anger. His hands curled, readying his claws. He could slice Jessica's throat in an instant.

"Corbin left information about the book at his house." The words tumbled out of Sebastian in a rush. "We need to go there to get it."

He felt Leon's attention shift to him. The sourness enveloped him. He felt an echo of Kobol's power and he realize that Kobol had turned Leon, so probably had a strong psychic link to him. An interesting way for Kobol to keep an eye on them.

"Maybe you should ask Kobol," Sebastian said. Or maybe you don't need to, he thought, leaving it unspoken. The anger drifted away. Indifference settled on Leon's face. It looked like his usual expression.

"We'll go," he said.

He drove them in a van similar to the one they'd been brought in. Instead of riding in the back, they shared the wide front seat. Sebastian noticed that the windows on the van had been replaced with blackout glass and inside the van, sheets of steel had been welded across in case the glass was broken. A van designed for a vampire to travel during the day, he realized. All they needed to do was infect someone enough to manipulate them. Or the quick and dirty way, just hire someone to drive and not tell them what was in the back.

He bet many drivers ended up as snacks that way.

They reached the mansion an hour before dawn. Leon jumped out of the van. In moments, he disabled the car Jessica and Sebastian had left in the driveway. No other vehicles were on the estate. Leon then returned to the van where Jessica and Sebastian waited.

"I will wait out the day in the van," he said. "If you find a lead, get moving on it. Do not bother trying to interrupt me during the day, the van locks from inside."

He handed the keys to Sebastian.

"Can I ask you a question?" Sebastian said.

Leon pulled the back door of the van open. He stopped and looked over.

"What is it?"

"How old where you when you were turned?"

A far away look come into Leon's pale blue eyes. He tilted his head. "I was nineteen, summering at my father's estate in the country."

"What year?" Jessica said.

Leon frowned. "I can't remember exactly. Fifteen something." He shrugged. "Get to work. You've only got one week." He climbed into the back of the van and locked the door.

"Fifteen something," Sebastian said.

"And he'd still be considered a somewhat young vampire," Jessica said. She slung the backpack over her shoulder and headed for the house. Sebastian followed.

They spent the morning digging a grave for Corbin and laying him to rest. When they finished patting down the last of the earth, Sebastian took the shovels back to the shed. He left Jessica standing by the grave, her hands curled into fists in her pockets, her head bowed. She held her shoulders rigid. He couldn't tell if she was crying.

Back in the house, he wandered through the hallways, peering into the rooms. The second fight had left even more of a mark on the house. Doorways shattered where the doors had been ripped away. Holes in the walls. Shattered glass and debris from broken furniture. He finished wandering the second floor and was about to head back to the first when he noticed a narrow door to the left of the back staircase. It was the only closed door in the house. He grabbed the door knob and turned. It resisted.

Locked.

Excitement surged through him. He didn't know why. Could the book be hidden behind this door? It couldn't be that easy, could it? Corbin had said he'd sent the book away.

He had to find a way to get the door open. It was a narrow door made from dark wood and intricately carved. It reminded Sebastian of a door to a pantry or something like that. Probably why no one had bothered with it, he thought. He bet Corbin would have designed it that way.

Without a key, he'd have to pick the lock. He retreated to an office farther down the hall and then returned with several paperclips. The lock was of a slightly different variety than he was used to and it took him a little longer to fit the paperclips in the right way. Some more fiddling... almost... there! He heard the soft click and the door knob turned in his hand.

He pulled the door open.

Narrow stairs led upward in total darkness. His eyes instantly adjusted, presenting the narrow walls and stairs in shades of grey. For a moment, he thought to call for Jessica and then decided not to bother her. Let her grieve in peace for a little while.

He started to move up the stairs. As he walked he noticed symbols drawn on the walls and etched into the stairs. He slowed to look at them. They weren't anything he recognized but he could feel power in them. It tingled on his skin and up his nerve endings. He felt the hair on his scalp standing on end. Part of him wanted to turn and run back down the stairs. Why was that, he thought then it came to him. Warding signs. These symbols were used to ward off vampires.

That was why they didn't bother with the door.

There was no way he could know that but he did. Something in him recognized these symbols and understood what they were. Was it because he was close to being a vampire? Even Corbin had said he'd come close, had even mistaken Sebastian for a vampire. Maybe he'd retained more of their characteristics than the other In-Between. Maybe that was why they didn't trust him.

The top of the stairs opened up into a small room. The angled ceiling told him this was in the attic at the top of the house, not a true third floor but a special hidden room. The floor and walls were lined with the same dark wood as the stairs and also like the stairs, were covered with the same carved symbols. Someone *really* didn't want any vampires to get into this room.

A plain metal desk sat in the corner. An old desktop computer complete with an old monitor sat on the desk. A narrow, four-drawer, filing cabinet sat opposite the desk. Sebastian crossed to the chair and turned on the computer. It fired up faster than he expected and automatically connected to a string of bulletin boards. It took a moment for him to realize what he was looking at and to find Corbin's handle. There it was: Razor.

He scrolled through several screens. Something about this was familiar to him. He'd seen it before but he hadn't looked at a computer in months. Hell, maybe even a year. Not since he'd left college. Not since...

His hand froze on the mouse. He heard Corbin's voice in his head again, as clear as when he'd spoken the words as he died. *Book. Find. Chat Stan. Book.*

Stan.

He remembered Stan. The basement apartment. The computer set up on a platform with three monitors. Stan folding his tall, thin body into the chair and pulling up a multitude of chat rooms for the In-Between. Pushing his thin granny glasses up his long nose as he peered at the screen. Long brown hair hanging over his shoulders. Thinking back, Sebastian remembered seeing Stan at Charlie's funeral, another figure in black standing at the edge of the grave. Just another mourner.

Who knew a little too much.

Had he kept digging after they left? Had Charlie's death sparked a desire to learn more? Had he figured out that the vampires the In-Between talked about wasn't some role-playing game but the real thing?

If he hadn't then, he would sure find out soon enough.

If they didn't find him first.

He dove into the computer, pulling up all of Corbin's messages. He had to figure out Stan's handle and from that he might be able to find out where the computer he was using was located. If Stan hadn't gone to the trouble of hiding it. He struck Sebastian as paranoid enough to do it but maybe he wouldn't have done it right away. Maybe once Sebastian found his handle, he could search the history to Stan's earliest messages and maybe from there find out where he was a year ago.

Or he could just return home and start from there.

He only had a week. He couldn't afford the flight time unless he was absolutely sure. Stick with the computer search for now.

He scrolled through screen shot after screen shot. Only when his shoulders began to ache and his head began to pound did he sit back, rubbing his eyes. He glanced at the computer time. Quarter to two.

Where had the morning gone? He'd found this room when, at eleven? Had he been staring at the screen this whole time? His sense of time was messed up. He felt like he'd only been up here for fifteen minutes and with no windows he couldn't tell how long. He checked his notes, scribbled on sheets of paper. He had several promising possibilities for Stan's handle but nothing definitive yet. Blurry eyed, he reviewed the list one last time: SamD, WilderOne, Yoda777, Frodo92 and LastByte. He ran a quick search and discovered that both Frodo92 and WilderOne were already posting almost two years ago. That meant they couldn't be Stan. Only three left. He remembered some Star Wars screensavers on Stan's computer which led him to lean more in favor of Yoda777 but he had to be sure. One last check.

More scrolling, more searching. He forced himself to keep blinking his eyes. His right shoulder ached. Just another few minutes and he would take a break.

He found the reference, buried in an introductory message from ten months ago. Almost two months after Charlie's death, as Sebastian recalled. Under the handle SamD the notation: Not Munster friendly. Then he remembered.

Stan had an image of Grandpa Munster on one of his computer screens.

Sebastian hit the search engine and pulled up information on Grandpa Munster, called Sam Dracula.

SamD.

Got ya!

He set the search parameters on the bulletin board and hit search. The computer flashed through, pulling up all of SamD's messages. They scrolled off the screen.

"Sebastian?"

Jessica's voice echoed from downstairs. He left the computer running and hurried down the stairs to the second floor. Mid afternoon sunlight blazing through the windows of the rooms as he passed made him squint. He reached the top of the stairs.

"Jessica!"

She appeared at the bottom and started up.

"Where have you been? I've been looking everywhere for you," she said. "I searched the library. There isn't anything there."

"I've been upstairs," he said. "Come on. I'll show you."

"There aren't any books up here," she said.

He took her arm and steered her down the hall. "No, I've been checking his computer."

"Computer? Corbin didn't have a computer."

"Yes he did," Sebastian said. "It just wasn't anywhere the vampires could get it."

He showed her the door. Her fingers traced the wood engravings. She took a few steps upward and stopped, staring at the walls.

"It feels weird," she said.

"I know," he said. "I think they're symbols to ward off vampires."

She glanced back at him.

"You feel it, don't you?"

She nodded. "I do. I think you're right."

She turned and climbed the rest of the stairs. He followed and again felt the same prickling along his skin and nerve endings. It was worse on the stairs as if they contained extra protection against vampires.

The small room felt even smaller with two of them in it. The arched, curving walls felt like they were pressing in on him. Just the symbols drawn on the walls, he thought and hurried over to the desk. He noticed Jessica hunched her shoulders as she followed him. If it affected her this way and she was less of a vampire than him, he imagined the vampires would never make it up these stairs. Would they even have seen the door, he wondered. That was an interesting thought.

As he sat in the computer chair, Jessica peered over his shoulder at the screen.

"What is that?" she said.

"A bulletin board for the In-Between," he said.

"What?"

"A computer bulletin board. The In-Between are using it to post about different topics. Look, reports on what works and what doesn't. Location reports. Private messages. That's what I've been looking for and tracking. Corbin mentioned the book as he died."

"Why didn't you say something?" she said.

"In front of Leon?"

"Right, of course. How did you know about this?"

"My friend Charlie had some of his friends scouring the Internet about what was happening to me," he said. "One of them contacted him and we went to see him. He had this same bulletin board on his screen." He swivelled the chair toward her. "Corbin mentioned his name as he died. He said "Book chat Stan." It made me think that he'd chatted with Stan."

"Stan, Charlie's friend?"

"Yeah."

"I don't see a Stan listed."

"He's not. He's using the handle SamD."

"And you think Corbin trusted him enough to give him the book?"

"Maybe it was a trade off between trusting him enough and trying to get the book somewhere no one would think to look for it."

She lifted her hip and perched on the side of the desk. Her leg hung down close to his own. If he moved his hand he could rest it on her thigh.

"So now what?" she said. "How do we find him?"

"We have to go home," he said. "To Ridgewater City."

She stiffened. "Do you really think Kobol will let us go there? Besides, how do you know Stan's still there? Maybe he came here to get the book?"

"I don't know," he said. "Not for sure."

"Then you'd better get sure. We've got a few more hours before Leon is up. I want some real progress by then."

"You're really going to give him the book? Just to get a shot at the vampire that turned Tommy?"

Her face was an impassive mask. "Just find it." Her body slipped off the desk and she stood up. He stood as well, blocking her against the desk, stopping her from leaving.

"Jessica, you know this is wrong. We can't just hand over this book. We don't even know what's in it."

"So we let Constantine get it first?" she said. "At least with Kobol's backing, we have a shot of finding it. He's got enough clout to keep the other vampires away from us while we search. None of those other clans will go against him."

"And then what happens when we find it? You really think he'll be all nice and do what we asked?"

"I think you either trust me or you don't," she said.

He didn't know what to say to that. After everything, he had to trust her. Didn't he? She'd always trusted him, supported him. Hadn't she earned his trust?

Her lips thinned as she waited. Finally she grabbed his arm to push him out of the way. He resisted, holding the edge of the desk, blocking her from moving past him.

"Damn you," she said. "You think you're the only one hurt by any of this?"

She shoved harder but he grabbed her waist and pulled her to him. Her hands grabbed his shoulders, nails digging in but he still wrapped his arms around her in an embrace. He felt her body rigid and unyielding against him, almost leaning away. Then she sagged, collapsing against him. Her hands held him to her instead of away. She pressed her face to his neck.

"I'm sorry," he said. "We'll find it. Then we'll deal with Kobol."

She shook her head. "No. You find it."

"What?"

She pulled away, looking him in the face. "You find it. Destroy it. You're right. We can't let any of them have it and none of the In-Between can keep it safe. I don't like what Frank's pages indicate and I don't like what Corbin said. A book made from human flesh just can't have anything good in it, nothing worth keeping. Whatever is in that book is evil and we can't keep it around."

"Wait a minute, what about what you said to Kobol? What about him keeping the other vampires off our backs?"

"They'll be off your back," she said, "and on mine. I'll lead them away from you. You go after the book."

"No way. I won't let you do that."

"It's the only way. Once I get rid of Leon, Kobol will come right after me. You have to be gone. You've got only about three hours before sundown. I'll kill Leon right before he rises and then I'll take the van."

"Jessica," he said.

"Don't argue. We don't have time. Find Stan. Get the book and destroy it."

"You?"

"I'll find you, don't worry about that."

"Liar," he said. "We'll go together. Take care of Leon now and take the van."

She shook her head. "Too obvious."

"It won't be obvious that we've split up?"

"Not if I kill you," she said.

"Um what?"

"I can stage it. Just as Leon wakes up. A gunshot from the house. I can run out and then shoot him with silver. Before he can recover, I cut off his head."

"That's crazy," he said. "You won't be able to do it. There aren't any guns left in the house."

"Not any down there." She pushed past him and moved to the filing cabinet. She slid open each drawer, checking inside. From the bottom one, she pulled out a black case. She set it on the floor and flipped it open. Inside, Sebastian saw pieces of a rifle. He blinked and she had half of it assembled. Another moment and she was finishing, snapping the final piece into place.

She opened the box of shells. He recognized the look of them. Home made silver, similar to the kind used by the In-Between.

"I knew Corbin would have one gun stashed away somewhere. It made sense it would be here, where the vampires wouldn't be able to get at it."

She stood up, holding the barrel down toward the floor.

"You have to go."

"How far am I going to get in two hours on foot?" he said. "I have a better idea."

"What's that?"

"We both go. Take the van, like Leon said, with him in the back. But we ditch it and take off."

"He'll come after us," she said.

"Not right away. Not if we disable the lock. It'll take him time to break out of there."

"Sebastian, you should go on your own."

He shook his head. "I'm not leaving you behind."

She sighed. "Fine. Where are we going?"

She packed up the rifle and they gathered the few silver weapons they could find into her backpack. He downloaded as much information from the bulletin boards as he could onto a flash drive and stuffed it in his pocket. As Jessica made a final sweep through the house, checking to see if there was anything else of possible use, he read through Frank's pages, trying to commit as much of it to memory as possible. At first, the squiggles and triangles still made no sense to him but then he realized they looked familiar. He squinted, holding them farther away.

"Jessica!"

He stood waiting by the front door. She appeared at the top of the stairs on the second floor.

"What is it?"

"The marks on these pages. I figured some of them out."

She hurried down the stairs. He met her just as she reached the bottom and held out the page to her.

"Look at this, the symbols. They look just like the ones on the walls of Corbin's office upstairs."

She held the sheet away from her. "You're right."

"I've got an idea," he said. "Did you see any markers?"

"I think there was something in the kitchen, for the white board on the fridge. Why?"

He pushed past her. "I've just thought of a way to keep Leon in the van."

Her eyes widened. "That's brilliant!"

She held the paper for him as he drew the symbols on the back doors of the van. When he finished, she compared them to the sheet and nodded.

"I'm going to do the sides as well."

"Good idea," she said. "Draw them in the back of the front cab too."

It took him a full hour to finish all around the van, even on the roof. He slid off, landing on his feet, sending up puffs of dust between his shoes. He brushed gravel off his hands.

He looked up to see Jessica grinning. She had her backpack slung over one shoulder and carried the rifle case in the other hand. She tilted her head, sending her ponytail swinging off her shoulder.

"Let's go," she said.

They climbed into the front of the van. The engine roared. Jessica hit the gas. The tires spun on the gravel then caught. They sped down the driveway.

"It finally feels like it's going our way," she said.

"I know what you mean," he said.

They reached the end of the driveway. She signalled to turn left.

A large black SUV raced forward, cutting them off. Tires squealed as the van skidded to a stop. Both Jessica and Sebastian were thrown forward. Sebastian felt the shoulder strap cut into his body as it held him back. Jessica's head smacked against the windshield.

So much for going their way.

CHAPTER TEN

The SUV stopped, still blocking them. Sebastian shook his head and focused. The doors to the SUV opened. Men wearing black jumped out.

"Jessica," he said. "In-Between."

She rubbed her head, smearing blood from a cut across her eyebrow. "What?" She turned to look. "Oh. Get the backpack."

They opened the van doors. The two men approaching stopped and crouched, whipping out hand guns from behind their backs. Both Jessica and Sebastian paused in the doorways.

"Come down slow," said the first man. "Step away from the vehicle."

He had an odd sounding accent, Sebastian thought. German maybe, or Scandinavian. Not a local group of In-Between. Had they been brought in because the local groups might have been contaminated by Jessica and Sebastian? He could see that as something the In-Between would think.

Stepping back from the door, he turned his head enough to watch Jessica. The two In-Between alternated their attention. When they shifted to her, Sebastian slung the backpack onto his shoulders.

"Hey, what are you doing?" said the odd accent man.

Sebastian held up his hands and stepped back. "Nothing."

"Come forward, toward me."

Sebastian took another step away, parallel to the side of the van. Over the trees across the road, he saw the last of the sun sending bursts of yellow and orange across the sky. Almost sundown.

He had an idea.

On the other side of the van, Jessica stepped forward. She stood in front of Odd Accent man. He took a step back from her, keeping her just out of jumping distance.

"Face the van. Put your hands on the hood."

"You mean on the boot?" she said.

"What?"

"The front here is the boot in England."

Sebastian took another two steps back.

"Whatever it is called, put your hands on it."

"I just want to do what you're telling me," Jessica said. "I just want to get it right."

Sebastian took another step. Almost to the end of the van now. Just one more step...

"Like this?" Jessica said. She put her hands behind her on the boot of the van.

"No, no, turn and face it," Odd Accent man said.

Sebastian ducked behind the van.

With his sleeve, he smeared and rubbed at the symbols on the door. The marker smudged but not enough. He kept rubbing. Come on, any second now and they'd realize he wasn't there and no distraction from Jessica would prevent them from heading here. He grabbed some dirt and rubbed it against the door. That helped. The symbols smeared and smudged beyond recognition.

"Hey, where are you?"

Sebastian ducked back around the end of the van. He held his arms up. "I had to take a leak."

The Odd Accent man frowned. "You are leaking?"

"I had to piss," Sebastian said. "You know? Relieve myself?"

The second man leaned forward and murmured in Odd Accent man's ear. Odd Accent man nodded.

"Enough. Come forward."

Sebastian walked toward the front of the van. Jessica stood leaning with both hands on the front end. Blood dripped from her forehead down her cheek. Her eyebrows raised in question. He gave her one slow blink, hoping she caught it in the fading light. She ducked her head. He saw the ghost of a smile on her lips.

"Stop there," said Odd Accent man. "Put your hands on the van." He frowned. "Take off the backpack."

Sebastian turned to the van and put his hands on the passenger's side windows. "Like this?"

"Take off the backpack."

Sebastian leaned farther forward and spread his legs a little. "This better?"

"The backpack," the man said. "Take it off your shoulders."

Long shadows reached from the trees across the road. The sky darkened even as Sebastian turned to look over his shoulder at the odd accented man.

"What about my shoulders?" he said.

"The backpack. Take it off!"

"Oh." Sebastian made a show of struggling with the backpack, making sure to kick his feet in the dirt, sending gravel spinning away. He grunted loud, even banged one arm against the door of the van, anything to make noise, to cover the click of the lock opening and the creak of the back door.

A sideways glance at the odd accented man told him he was pushing his luck. He allowed the backpack to slide off his arms. It landed in the dirt. Sebastian turned back to the van and put his hands on the sides by the window. Odd Accent man lifted his gun.

"Now, where are you going?" he said.

A snarl sounded from above them.

Odd Accent man looked up just as Leon sailed over the side of the van. He crashed into the man. The gun flew away. Leon lifted a hand, claws glinted in the twilight.

The second man shouted and fired. The bullets struck Leon, knocking him sideways. He fell, snarling.

Sebastian grabbed the backpack and ducked forward. Jessica had spun around the second man and shoved him forward. He stumbled, falling to his knees. Leon leapt up, snarling. He raced forward. Jessica scooped up the fallen gun and ran to the black SUV.

Sebastian raced around the front, heading for the passenger's side. For a moment, he felt a twinge of guilt leaving these men with Leon then the gun sounded. The second man shot Leon in the chest, pushing him back. As Sebastian jumped in the seat, he saw Odd Accent man swing a blade at Leon's neck. Leon ducked and backhanded the man. Jessica then hit the accelerator and the SUV spun away, heading down the road into the darkness.

"Can you see?" Sebastian said. "Your head."

"It's fine," she said. "Buckle up. I want to get as much distance from here as possible."

He buckled himself in and then helped her slide her buckle into the lock.

"So much for trapping Leon," he said.

"Those In-Between will keep him busy," she said. "But you know what that means?"

"What?"

"They'll be after us too. We were working with a vampire. It won't matter why. They'll hunt us down to kill us now."

"Great," Sebastian said. "So you're telling me we've got vampires and In-Between after us now?"

"Yep."

"Because of some book that we don't even know the purpose of."

"That's right."

"Why was it such a good idea to come to Europe?"

She shrugged. "Didn't you tell me once you always wanted to travel?"

⚜

They'd been driving for an hour when he finally asked where they were going.

"Airport," she said. "Manchester International. I know a safe house about an hour away. We can get money and ID, book a flight."

"An In-Between safe house?" he said. "How can you be sure they won't turn us in?"

In the faint light from the headlights, he saw a muscle along her jaw flex.

"They know me," she said and refused to say anything more.

He turned to stare out the window, watching the flashes of trees and buildings speed by. When had it all gone so wrong? No, wrong question. Had it ever been right? Instead of camaraderie and acceptance from the In-Between, he'd received only suspicion and avoidance. Anything they'd taught him had been at Jessica's insistence. Even now he wasn't sure why but he had some inklings. Until he met Corbin and had the man tell him outright that he'd mistaken Sebastian for a vampire, he hadn't realized just how different he was from the other In-Between. His constant headaches from the sun, his more enhanced psychic abilities. He was that much closer to an actual vampire. Maybe all he needed was another taste from Bianca and he would fall all the way.

But he would never let that happen. He'd never take that step. All he had to do was think of Charlie and Alexa and any temptation vanished. He wouldn't be like Alexa, and he wouldn't do what she'd done to Charlie.

So he would have to find a way to survive, and it looked like he'd have to do it without the In-Between. The thought didn't feel so bad. They'd all just tolerated each other. Leaving them behind meant nothing. As long as...

He started to turn but stopped and focused out the window. As long as Jessica stayed with him, he knew it would be okay. He knew *he* would be okay, and he'd do whatever he had to to make sure she was safe.

When had that become so important?

He didn't know. Couldn't remember when it had crept up on him. She'd always been around and he just... expected it. Now he owed her for it, for everything. She'd turned her back on her friends, on the people who had helped her and trained her and sheltered her for years, all for him.

He wouldn't let it be a waste.

This book, they had to find this book and figure out why it was so important, to the vampires and to the In-Between. Why had Morgan sat on Frank's notes this whole time? Why did those squiggles and triangles feel so familiar? It wasn't just seeing them drawn and carved into the stairway and office at Corbin's house, it was something else. Something inside him stirred when he looked at those symbols.

He leaned his head back against the headrest and closed his eyes. What would that book look like, he wondered. Would it be a hard back cover, made of leather, or soft like cardboard? No, not soft. Hard, with a black finish, smooth and silky. He could feel the texture under his fingers. It would feel warm, absorbing and reflecting back the heat in his hands. The book was large, almost twice the width of his hands. The pages were aged, almost brown, edges frayed in spots, a few tears. On some of the pages were large blotches of something long since dried into a darker brown stain.

Small handwriting covered the pages in black marks. The language was one he'd never seen before and he wasn't even sure it was human. Did anyone make marks in that way to have any kind of meaning? They contained things that no human would think to record. He sensed tales of blood and power in these symbols, calls to deeper, darker forces that dwelled many years ago, invocations to unbind them.

His fingers stroked the pages but now his fingers were thick, heavy skinned with long, curved claws. He licked out a forked tongue to wet his finger and turn the page. As his hand touched it, he felt the life essence in the page, the flesh of a human stretched and cured to be bound in this book, just as the essence was bound in the pages, giving a living sacrifice to the symbols and words within.

He dipped the point of his stylus into the bowl of ink made from countless drops of countless victims, stirred and replenished over years, mixed with other concoctions to achieve the black color. Then he pressed the point to page and began to write.

Write of the future history to come of all the vampires of the world and how they would grow to devour all and how one would arise to defeat them. Write of the remembrance of flesh, of bone, of blood dripping, boiling, stirring, flowing like rivers into open mouths. Write of the dissolution of emotion, dribbling away all concern, all humanity rotting and stinking, left only to fill the need, feed the hunger that was never ending...

"Sebastian... Sebastian!"

A voice called from far away. The book began to dissolve. He tried to grasp it, tried to hold onto it but it rotted, pieces falling and scattering in a breeze that blew but that he could not feel. The pieces shattered, fragments disappearing into the distance.

"SEBASTIAN!"

Pain stung his face. He felt something rough on his cheek, grinding into his skin. Where was the seat? The SUV? He wasn't in the passenger's seat anymore. His eyes opened. Darkness still, night still. He could feel it in his bones. The cool, welcoming embrace of the night. For the past year he'd only felt fully comfortable at night.

He was lying on the ground. He tried to push himself up. His hands (strange, human hands with no claws) shifted on the gravel. His body (smaller, thinner, without the feeling of coursing power) shuddered and jerked as he tried to sit up. Now other hands grabbed his shoulders, steadying him, helping him until he leaned against the wheel behind him.

Jessica crouched in front of him. Worry creased lines into her face.

"Are you all right?" she said. Her hand reached out and brushed his black hair off his forehead.

With every breath, he felt more inside his own body again, felt the reality of this place. The gravel under his hands. The hardness of the ground beneath his legs. The press of the rubber wheel against his back. The softness of Jessica's hand as she brushed the hair from his eyes.

He wished he could smell her.

He opened his mouth, experimenting to see if he could still control that part of himself, still talk. The jaw seemed to work. Next try sounds.

"I... I okay." His voice sounded garbled.

Jessica didn't look convinced by this pronouncement.

"What happened?" he said.

"You started convulsing, that's what happened," she said. "We were driving along and all of a sudden you're spasming in your seat. I had to pull over. I could barely get you out of the car, you were shaking and jerking so much."

"Convulsing?" He didn't remember that. He closed his eyes and rubbed his temples with his fingers. What did he remember?

Something about the book. Something about flesh.

His hands...

"I'm hungry," he said.

She frowned. "Okay. There's a pub a few miles down."

She helped him stand. He still felt odd in his body, as if he wasn't used to these dimensions anymore. He took a few steps, holding onto the SUV but shaking off her hand. With each placement of his foot, he felt more grounded, more sure of himself as himself. Yes, this was right. That other before (whatever it was) was the odd one. This was his self.

He straightened, letting go of the SUV. Now he felt solid.

"Okay," he said. "Let's go."

The creases of worry still lined her face. "Can you tell me anything about it?" she said. "Did you fall asleep?"

"I don't know." He tried to grasp the last vestiges of image as it dissolved in his mind. The book? But he could no longer be sure if he'd actually thought of it before or was just thinking of it now. He shook his head.

"Okay." She patted his shoulder. "Let's get something to eat."

He climbed back into the SUV. With a final glance at him, she started it back up and soon they were driving down the road. She turned off onto a side street, driving for several blocks. Familiar buildings, most three or four story shops, now dark, lined the street. At the corner, he spotted a pub. When he pointed, she nodded and pulled the SUV into a parking spot across the street.

When she shut the car off, she sat back and looked at him. "You got any money?"

"Um, not much."

"Right. Follow my lead then. Let me do the talking."

"Okay."

They piled out of the SUV and headed across to the pub. Faded paint on the walls and door betrayed its age. The door creaked but opened smoothly as they pushed their way through. Inside, a steady din of talking and music filled the space. The overwhelming scent of humans struck him in the face. He almost physically recoiled. It had been so long since he'd been in such a large crowd of regular people. He'd forgotten the stink of them.

Jessica glanced at him and gave him a shake of her head. He nodded back. Control. He had to remember to stay in control. Beneath the smell of cologne and sweat, he could smell the sweetness of blood. So much of it here, all of it so accessible.

Control.

He followed Jessica to a small table by the wall, halfway into the pub. There were no empty tables closer to the door. At least they were by a wall. Just brace against it. He could handle it. Just stayed focused. Remember why he was here. Get some food and get out.

A waitress walked up, pen poised over pad. "Can I help you folks?"

"Can we get a menu?" Jessica said. "And we'll have two half pints of Guinness."

"Right, love." The waitress scribbled and turned away. She swiped a couple of menus from two tables over, eliciting yells from the patrons. She yelled back and they shut up. She dropped the menus on the table in front of Jessica.

"I'll be back with your drinks." She walked off.

"I don't think I should drink anything," Sebastian said.

"Just let it sit in front of you then," Jessica said. "This is a pub. People come in to drink. It would look weird not to have a drink in front of you." She slid a menu across to him. "Pick something."

He flipped it open. "Burger, rare."

"Me too."

He closed the menu and tried to keep his gaze fixed on it, but the feel of all these people around him drew his gaze upward. He looked around. People lined the bar across, some leaning, others poised on stools. People crowded around the tables near the door, raising glasses to drink, talking, hands moving, voices loud with laughter. At the back of the pub, he noticed a dart board with several men tossing darts and chiding each other on their skill or lack of it. Waitresses with white aprons tied to their waists slipped through the crowd, hoisting massive trays filled with glasses. He inhaled the moist smell of yeasty malt and hormones, all just a slim coating over the sweet smell of blood.

"You having trouble?" she said.

Her voice jolted him. "What? No."

"Don't lie to me," she said. "You haven't looked this itchy since the first couple of months. What's going on?"

Before he could respond, the waitress reappeared. She set down two glasses of Guinness in front of them, then wiped her hand on her apron. "Any decisions?"

"We'll have two burgers, extra rare," Jessica said. She slid the menu back to the waitress.

Sebastian pulled the beer closer to him, letting the heady scent fill his nostrils. It helped drown out the smell of the waitress's blood. She was a smoker, he could tell, balanced on the edge of cancer. The stench of almost-sickness gave her blood a sour smell but it wouldn't affect the taste.

God, what the hell was wrong with him?

He forced himself to sip the Guinness. As usual, it had no flavor, just a warm slimy feel down his throat. But it did stop him from attacking the waitress.

Jessica stared at him. "What is with you?"

He swallowed. "I don't know. There's so many people in here."

"You've been in crowds before," she said. "It's been a long time since you reacted like this."

"I don't know. The book..."

"Book?"

The word shuddered through his mind. "I dreamed of the book." The words were out of his mouth before he even knew he'd thought them. He looked up to see the creases of worry etched in her face again. He seemed to worry her more and more these days.

"Am I getting worse?" he said.

"Worse? What do you mean?"

"Corbin thought I was a vampire. The other In-Between..."

She shook her head. "Forget them. It was close for you, Sebastian. Maybe closer than anyone else they've met but you're still an In-Between.

You aren't a vampire and as long as you don't do anything stupid, you'll stay an In-Between."

She meant do anything stupid, like drink blood.

He took another sip of beer.

The waitress returned with their burgers. He inhaled the scent of the warm meat. He cut into it with a knife, relishing the bright redness inside. Very rare, just warmed on the grill. As usual, it had no flavor but at least he felt the warmth of it in his mouth.

"What was this dream?" Jessica said. She fiddled with her burger, adding ketchup and mustard as if she could taste it.

"I don't really remember." He took another bite. The warmth of the burger and the sips of beer helped settle his nerves. His shoulders sagged with relief. At least he didn't feel like leaping at the people at the next table anymore.

"Was that what you were dreaming about in the car?" Jessica said. "Before..." She stopped, glancing at the crowds around them. "Before I pulled you out?"

He tried to remember. What was he dreaming? He didn't even remember falling asleep but he must have if he woke up again. But it wasn't like any sleep he'd ever had before. He looked down at the half eaten burger on his plate. Beside it, a thick fingered hand with huge yellowing claws lay halfway between the plate and the beer glass. All it needed was the bowl of blood ink and a stylus to write onto the pages of the book.

He jolted back in his chair. His hand hit the beer glass, tipping it but Jessica's super fast reflexes grabbed and righted it before a drop spilled.

"Sebastian, you've gone white. What is it?"

"My hand..." How could he explain it? He didn't even understand it himself.

She looked at his hand and then back at him. "What about it?"

"It... it wasn't mine."

She frowned. "What do you mean not yours? Whose was it?"

"Grellock." The word came out of his mouth before he even realized he'd spoken.

Now Jessica's face turned white, as if all the blood in her body drained out of her within seconds.

"Who's that?" Sebastian said.

"I think it might..." she said. "I'm not sure."

"Best guess."

"I think that was the name of the first vampire."

He pushed the half finished burger away. "I have to get out of here."

"Sebastian..."

"I mean it, there's too many people. I can't..." He stood up from the table, bumping his leg on the chair. It teetered but he grabbed it and pushed it back under the table.

"I'll meet you at the car." He turned and pushed into the crowd.

Oh bad idea, he realized as the smells of the people enveloped him. Deodorant, hair spray, gel, cologne, after shave, perfume, sweat, body odor, tooth paste, beer, frying oil, chips, all assailed him but none of it could cover the sweet lingering aroma of blood. He felt the pull of it, the call to drink, just a little, just one mouthful, one single drop. Its siren song purred to him, inviting him, encouraging him but he knew the danger. Had seen it when Alexa fell on Charlie and ripped out his throat.

Alexa...

She'd been here.

He stopped almost to the door. He could feel the trace of her. Not a scent, but almost a vibration. If he tried to listen, tried a little harder to feel it... yes, right there. He turned toward the booths along the wall. She'd been there.

And she hadn't been alone.

He had only been in Constantine's presence a couple of times but it had imprinted on him. He'd know it anywhere, and Constantine had been here. He'd been here with Alexa. Some time ago, but fairly recently. A few weeks maybe? He couldn't tell anything more than that.

Jessica pushed through the crowd and grabbed his arm. "Sebastian, what's going on?"

"They met here," he said.

"Who did?"

"Alexa and Constantine. They were here."

"They're here?" Jessica surveyed the crowd. "I don't smell them."

"They aren't here now but they were here. A while ago. Maybe a few weeks. Maybe shorter."

"How do you know that?"

"I feel it."

He looked down at her. Her eyes widened. For the first time, since he'd met her, he saw fear in her eyes.

Fear of him.

CHAPTER ELEVEN

She didn't say anything as they piled into the SUV and drove. He didn't say anything either. What could he say? She was afraid of him. Maybe it was time for her to go.

But he didn't want her to.

Was that selfish? He'd lost everything: Alexa, Charlie, his family, his future. She was the only thing he had left. What would happen to him if she left? Even considering it made his chest ache.

She pulled into a residential neighbourhood and parked on the street. When she turned off the engine, he could see the beginning rays of sunlight peeking over the clouds in the distance.

"This is what we're going to do," she said. "We're going to find that damn book. We're going to burn it. We're going to kill Kobol or anyone else who gets in our way and then we're getting the hell out of here. Got that?"

He nodded. "Just one question."

"What?"

"Can we go to Australia? I at least speak the language down there."

She stared at him for a moment and then burst into laughter. He heard the tinge of hysteria on the edges but it didn't matter. At least she'd laughed. At least she'd said 'we.'

"Jessica," he said.

She wiped tears of laughter from her face and hiccupped. "Yeah?"

"Thanks for sticking around."

She quieted down. "Why wouldn't I?"

She turned toward the door but he reached over, pulling her by the waist toward him. She turned in surprise and he kissed her. His hand plunged into the mass of her ponytail, feeling the softness caress his palm as her lips caressed his and his hand held her head. Her arms wrapped around him as he pressed her to him. Finally they stopped for breath.

"Just my luck," she said.

"What?"

"To go for the freak who even the other freaks think is freaky."

Go for, she'd said go for. He felt a warmth spread through his chest. He traced the line of her cheek with his fingers. "I never thought I'd go for an older woman."

She swatted his hand away. "Jerk." But a small smile curled her lips.

And at least she didn't look afraid of him.

For the moment.

They got out of the SUV. She retrieved her backpack and slung it over her shoulder as she led him across the street. He glanced back at the SUV and noticed the No Parking sign next to it.

"Shouldn't we move the car?" he said.

"We won't be using it again," she said. "I'll have someone take care of it."

He caught up to her as she started past the row houses. Dark windows faced the street, shuttered against them.

"Are you sure we can trust this safe house?" he said.

"Are you doubting my judgment?" she said.

"No."

"Then relax. Not every In-Between is going to listen to Nigel and his friends."

She stopped at a small chain link fence and unhitched the gate. The links tinkled as she pushed the gate open. He slipped in after her, closing it as she headed up the cobblestone path. The small row house looked just like any other, red brick with grey shutters closed against the night. A dark grey door sat sensibly closed until Jessica stepped up. She raised her hand to knock but the door was already opening.

A tall woman with greying hair cut in a bob at her chin gestured them in, stepping back to allow entrance. Sebastian felt the cool appraisal in her hazel eyes as he slipped by. She closed the door and led them through the dark toward the light shining from a back room. They stepped into a kitchen decorated in soft butter yellow shades. The woman pulled out the chairs around a table.

"Thank you for letting us in, Joan," Jessica said.

A smile flickered across the woman's face. "I thought I might be seeing you, Jessica." They embraced.

When Jessica pulled back she turned to Sebastian. "This is Sebastian, another In-Between. Sebastian, this is Joan."

"Nice to meet you," Sebastian said.

"I hope I can say the same," Joan said. "I've heard things about you, about the raid in Calais."

"That wasn't his fault," Jessica said.

"I didn't say I believe it but I do reserve judgment to see for myself." She turned to a kettle on the counter. Jessica sat at the table and motioned Sebastian to sit. He did so, although he wasn't so thrilled to be accused by someone he'd never met. The In-Between grapevine had been working overtime. He'd known it would be like this but he still didn't like it. He'd been the one to say there were more vampires. If Morgan had listened to him...

Enough. He'd done what he could to help. He'd tried to fit in but they hadn't accepted him because he was just a little too close to being a vampire. He couldn't help that and he couldn't change it.

The woman turned, setting tea cups and a plate of biscuits in front of them. Soon a kettle of steeping tea sat in the center and the woman pulled her own chair back. She settled in.

"So tell me about this book," she said.

Sebastian, reaching for a biscuit, froze with his hand hovering over the plate. The bland, curious expression on the woman's face gave nothing away. Even Jessica seemed nonplussed by the comment.

"You didn't tell him about me, I see," Joan said.

"No," Jessica said. "I wasn't even sure you'd let us in."

A smile curled the woman's lips, crinkling lines around her mouth and in the corners of her eyes. "You know better than that, Jessica."

"I'd hoped, but I didn't want to presume."

Joan reached across and squeezed her hand. "As long as you don't lie to me you know you're welcome here."

She released Jessica's hand and turned to Sebastian. "As for you, we'll see if that's the case, shall we?"

"Who are you?" Sebastian said.

Joan laughed. "You mean 'what,' don't you?"

His cheeks warmed. He pulled his hand back from the biscuits.

"I have a special talent for picking up on things, you might say," Joan said. "That's why I'll reserve judgment about you. Even if you did come here by way of the vampires."

Her gaze shifted to Jessica. Jessica looked right back, calm and assured. So she'd been expecting this. Would have been nice to have been warned.

Joan's gaze shifted back to him. Now it felt like being under a spotlight. How deep did she see into him?

"The book," she said. "Tell me about it."

He shrugged. "It's old. Corbin said it was written by the first vampire on human flesh and it's supposed to be magic. Foretells the end of the world."

She nodded. "Yes, that's what he knew about it. What do you know about it?"

He felt her words sink into him. Her tone, pitched low and smooth, echoed in his head: *what do you know about it?* He felt the words vibrate inside him. Her hazel eyes widened and began to fill his vision. He felt the lids of his own eyes droop. His muscles relaxed. His shoulders sagged. He slumped back in his chair but it wasn't a kitchen chair anymore. Instead it was a large, wood-carved throne of a chair. Heavy, the arms carved with intricate figures and stained with the spillage of blood and other secretions. His thick hands lay flat on a marble topped table, on either side of a large bladed knife. Across the way, the darkness hid a large figure. A creature with burning red eyes. Not of this world, he knew it somehow, from the Netherworld, summoned by his incantations and sacrifices over many, many weeks and months. So many sacrifices, first all the animals, then the villagers and finally his family. The screams of his wife and children echoed in his mind, music to this creature, even as their blood nourished and called him forth into the physical realm.

"I want to live forever," he told this creature.

You will, the creature's response rumbled in his mind. *But you will pay the price in blood.*

Hands reached across the marble topped table. Fingers of impossible length, covered in sores and dripping pus that hissed and stained the marble as it splattered. Fingers that split and oozed even as they reached, bones and claws breaking through flesh as if the creature wasn't quite able to hold onto its physical self. Reaching, reaching, to touch, to infect.

Reaching.

He hit the floor. Butter yellow walls loomed over him. He felt his legs tangled in the kitchen chair. His hands pressed against the tile floor. His hands, regular thin fingers, not the thick fingers with yellow claws or the impossible long fingers reaching.

Just his own.

"Sebastian!" Jessica pushed back her chair and hurried to him.

He felt her hands on his shoulders, helping him sit up. He blinked and shook his head, trying to orient himself back in this room, in this kitchen. His legs shook as he stood up. Jessica helped him right the chair and he slumped into it.

"I'm okay," he said, testing his voice. It was his own, thank god.

"You're connected to it," Joan said. "Have you ever seen the book?"

Jessica moved away from in front of him, staying by his side. He felt her hand on his shoulder.

"No," he said. "I've never seen it."

The woman frowned. "You're closer to the change than any other In-Between. You're connected to the book. That makes you dangerous."

"He's not dangerous," Jessica said.

"He is," Joan said. "He feels the book, even stronger than the vampires. They're too close to its source, they can't feel it because it's too close to them but he's just far enough away to have a better look. That's why you can't fit in with the other In-Between. They feel it in you too. And the vampires know that you can find the book. That's why they're hunting you."

Sebastian felt Jessica's hand tighten on his shoulder. "What can I do?" he said.

"Run," Joan said. "Get as far away as possible. You need to stay away from that book."

"Why?" Jessica said. "Frank's notes indicate it can do something about the clan heads. Corbin thought it was important too. Why can't we use that book against the vampires?"

"You know, don't you?" Joan said to Sebastian.

Unease curled in his stomach, clenching the muscles. He did know, felt it in the icy flow of his blood in his veins, in the way he hungered when he smelled people now more than ever. Even Joan now. He could smell her above the subtle scent of Earl Grey tea.

To use that book he would have to touch it, to open it and if he did that...

He remembered dripping pus hissing as it hit marble.

Infected.

"It could turn us," he said. "First the In-Between and then the regular people."

Jessica looked startled. "What are you talking about? A book can't infect people."

"This book can."

Jessica turned to Joan. The woman nodded. "He's seen it."

"What the hell are you talking about?" Jessica said. "Joan, I know you can see things some times but this is crazy. I don't know what's in this book but I know that two men I trusted and respected thought it could help. I'm not going to let the vampires get it." She patted Sebastian's shoulder. "Come on, let's go. This isn't the place I thought it was."

"I'm sorry, Jessica." Joan pushed her chair back from the table but instead of stepping forward, she stepped back, angling away from them.

"What?"

A soft thump from the front of the house interrupted Jessica. Sebastian heard a hiss. Through the doorway down the hall, he saw the first wisps of gas. He grabbed Jessica's arm. "Run!"

"This way!" She shoved a chair at the back door and darted into the hallway. Sebastian followed. She raced into the closest room and crossed it two leaps, heading for the window. Sebastian caught a whiff of vapor as he followed her into the room. He slammed the door shut as a coughing fit took hold. Back against the door, the coughing wracked his body, forcing him to double over. His eyes watered. Rawness ached in his throat. A hand grabbed his arm and yanked him forward.

"Come on!" Jessica shoved.

He felt the edges of the window frame. He climbed out, dropping the few feet to a path running along the side of the house. Early morning sunlight brightened the sky. Not vampires.

Joan had betrayed them to the In-Between.

"Catch!" Jessica leaned out the window, holding the backpack. He held out his arms as she tossed it. He caught it and slung it over his shoulder.

"Come on, Jessica."

Her head ducked back in. Her leg appeared through the window then he heard the splinter of shattering wood. She yelled. Her leg was wrenched back into the room.

"Jessica!"

"Run!" He heard her scream. A shadow crossed the window. Then a man stuck his head out.

Nigel.

Sebastian ran.

At first he thought they would catch him. There seemed to be so many of them and they seemed to be everywhere but the more he ran the more he realized that he could slip away from them, that their numbers were fewer than he'd realized. Soon he couldn't hear anyone following him as he hurried down a side street.

He wanted to circle back and see if he could rescue Jessica but he knew they'd expect that of him. She would be heavily guarded if only because of her relationship to him. Never mind her betrayal, as they'd see it.

There was only one way he could secure her release.

Find the book.

The one thing he didn't want to do because he knew what it meant. He'd known it from the look in Corbin's eyes, the reactions of the other In-Between, even Kobol's acknowledgement of him as an almost vampire. Sebastian was as close as he could get without crossing over, but that bridge was very short. It wouldn't take much to cross it.

Maybe just a few simple pages.

But there was no other way. He had to find it and find it before the vampires and the In-Between. They had so many more resources than him, so many more people scouring the country but he had a few things they didn't have. He knew Stan had it and he almost felt a connection to the book. A connection that if he worked on it, would bring him closer and closer to the book.

He just had to make sure he remembered who he was when he found it.

CHAPTER TWELVE

The bright morning sun pierced his eyes and pounded in his temples as he walked the streets. The last of the In-Between's drug was well gone from his system and now his reaction to daylight returned in full force. It hadn't been this bad since he'd first been infected. Even the skin on his arms felt like it was sizzling in the sunshine.

Was England supposed to have such bright sunlight? Whatever happened to the fog filling the streets in perpetual twilight? *That* he could handle. But instead he was stuck with this light.

And without Jessica.

Stop thinking about her. Every time he let her into his mind, his chest ached. He felt like he'd let her down. She'd wanted him to fit in and he'd tried so hard. Despite what he knew now he still felt like he'd failed her.

He couldn't fail her again.

The book. Where was the book?

Even with that casual thought, he felt it prickle inside his mind. He felt himself turn toward it, like a magnet pulled north. Could it really be that simple, to just follow the call in his head? A part of him still felt the need to search the Internet, look in maps and try all the mundane normal search methods but now with the pull of the book he knew he didn't need them. He could find the book easily.

It called to him now.

And why now all of a sudden, he wondered, even as his feet made a turn around the corner without him being aware of it. Why had the book become... active?

Stan had opened it.

Maybe he wasn't the first one. Maybe that had been Corbin or one of the other In-Between, but someone somewhere had woken the book up and with each turn of the pages, the book became more and more awake until now it was awake enough to reach out and call. Did the vampires hear the call the way he did? He didn't know but Joan had said they were too close to it. They didn't feel the book the way he did.

But maybe it was only a matter of time, maybe the more the book was opened, the stronger it reached out until even the vampires would feel it.

He didn't have much time.

He had to find a car. He could feel the pull of the book drawing him southeast. It had to be in London and he had to find a way to get there. Maybe a car wasn't such a good idea. He'd never really gotten the hang of driving on the left side of the road. How else could he get there?

Train.

He didn't like the confinement of a train but he didn't have much choice, not if he didn't want to risk driving and being a danger to himself and anyone else unfortunate enough to be on the road with him. It couldn't take more than a few hours to get to London, could it? All he had to do was find the train station.

All he had to do was figure out what city he was in.

He hurried down the street with the sun pounding at his head. Ahead he noticed a vegetable and fruit market. Large stalls presented an array of fruits, oranges, apples, pears. Heads of lettuce and peppers mixed with cucumbers. A few women poked around the stalls. He slipped past them. As soon as he walked under the shade of the awning, he relaxed. Ahh, even a slight shadow gave him some relief from the blistering sun. A woman holding an orange gave him an odd look. He turned away from her. The scent of the orange gave her blood a richer scent. He didn't want to focus on that.

He stepped inside the shop and was presented with an immediate challenge that he would certainly have to deal with on the train.

At least five people stood inside, scattered in the shop looking at different fruits and vegetable displays. At the back, the owner stood behind the counter, ringing up a customer. The short, squat man with large hands bagged the tomatoes and mushrooms, then exchanged the bag for money. Thanking the customer, he wiped his hands on his white apron as he surveyed the shop.

The lady customer strolled past Sebastian. He caught a whiff of the ripe tomatoes, one just on the edge of turning bad, but none of it able to hide the scent of her blood.

If he decided to travel by train he would have to deal with being surrounded by people, by being surrounded by the scent of the their blood.

What choice did he have?

At least he could go to the train station. Surely there'd be lots of people there and he could test himself to see if he could stand it. If not, there were bound to be lots of cars he could choose from.

Maybe he would even be able to persuade someone to drive him.

Like that wouldn't pose any more of a challenge, being in the close quarters of a car smelling the blood of one person and opposed to a large train car filled with people.

One step at a time.

He headed down the aisle, past the broccoli and cauliflower, toward the counter. As he stepped up, the squat man placed his hands on the counter near the till.

"Can I help you?"

Sebastian could smell the scent of suspicion on the man. Understandable. Sebastian had walked up without any fruits or vegetables.

"Can you tell me where the train station is? I'm a bit lost."

The man nodded. "I'll say you are, mate. Got a bit of a walk to get to Lime Street Station. It's a big dome of a building. Head out here and turn right. Go five lights east and then turn left about a quarter... let me draw it for ya."

He pulled out a paper bag and sketched a quick map in black pencil, marking the shop and the station with big Xs. As he handed the bag to Sebastian, Sebastian smelled the sourness in his blood. The man was ill, with something serious.

"Thanks," Sebastian said. "You should see a doctor. You aren't well."

The man frowned in puzzlement. "Eh?"

"Trust me. Thanks again for this." Sebastian turned away from the man before he could say anything. He almost bumped into a woman behind him. The flare of her nostrils only underlined the sweetness of her blood.

"Sorry," he murmured and slipped past her. He moved quickly to get out of the store even though he didn't relish being back in the sunshine again.

But as he stepped outside he found a few clouds had drifted across the sky, hiding the sun and creating shadows. Relief. He turned right as the fruit seller suggested and started walking.

So was he going to be able to do it? Would he be able to ride the train to London without losing control? He had no way to know. The only way to even test the theory would be to hang around the train station around people and see how it went. Maybe he could develop a tolerance, be able to ignore them.

And maybe pigs would fly.

He managed to screw up the directions once but it only added a few minutes to the walk. It was still almost noon by the time he reached the train station. As he approached it, he could almost feel the hum of life inside. As the fruit vendor had said, the station was a large dome made of glass, or at least it appeared that way to Sebastian. Damnit even inside he would be subjected to sunlight. He pushed through the large double doors. The brightness felt blinding. His head throbbed.

Around him the smells of people assailed him from all sides with the sweet undercurrent of blood. He ducked away from one group of people only to find himself too close to two women reviewing a time table. He hurried past them, trying to maintain his equilibrium. Too many people in here, what the hell were they all doing at the train station in the early afternoon? Didn't these people have jobs?

He noticed a long curving line of people to buy tickets from an array of slotted windows. God, he'd never be able to stand being in that crowd for more than a minute without snapping. But he had to get a ticket to London. There had to be some kind of automated machine.

And of course there would be and it would take credit cards.

Which he didn't have.

He had to face the line so he could talk to a clerk and persuade him to hand over a ticket for next to nothing. He checked his pockets. No, make that nothing. No machine would do that.

Bracing himself, he headed for the back of the line, following a young woman carrying a toddler in her arms. She pushed an empty stroller ahead of her, a large bag strapped to the back of the stroller and her own back. The child smelled of talcum and strained peas. It stared with wide brown eyes over the woman's shoulder at Sebastian. Soon Sebastian could smell the child's blood, fresh and warm, under the smell of powder.

He would never be able to stand this. What could he do? He picked at the backpack straps on his shoulders. He gazed across the great expanse of the station but everywhere he looked were people. Standing, walking, talking, gesturing, checking cell phones, chiding children, waving to someone across the way and all of them smell of warm, fresh, delicious blood.

He had to get out of here. But he had to get that ticket first. Then what? Even if he managed to get a ticket, could he really control himself all the way to London? There had to be something he could do, some way he could distract himself.

He thought of the book.

It felt like an itch in his mind, a call tugging at him. When he focused on it, the temptation of the blood around him faded, drowned out by a stronger urge. But even as he focused on it he could tell that it was stronger, that his attention gave it strength and pulled him more insistently. But he wanted to find it, didn't he? So wasn't it okay to pay attention to it?

He knew it wasn't that simple. That paying attention to it didn't just give it strength but gave it power over him, but now the desire for blood had almost vanished. How could he not use this as a way to protect himself and the people around him?

The line moved forward. He pulled his attention from the book and focused on the floor. The smell of blood came back to him but it was a trace of itself, a tease. Maybe he could just give the book a little attention and that would help him through. But he still couldn't keep waiting.

He tapped the woman on the shoulder. She turned and the toddler wiped his head around to stare at Sebastian as the woman faced him.

"Yes," the woman said.

"I really need to get to London," Sebastian said. "You will let me in front of you." He allowed his voice to give an inflection of command. The woman's expression changed from curiosity to a slackness that spread across her features, leaving them looking loose. Her eyes defocused.

"Of course." Her voice slurred as she spoke.

He slipped past her and tapped the man in front on the shoulder. When he turned, Sebastian repeated his request and command. The man resisted and it took a second request before his features loosened and his eyes slid away from Sebastian.

The next few people succumbed easily and Sebastian moved through the line. Soon he was next, standing behind an old lady. The desire to push past her was strong but he let her go. He wanted to conserve his energy for the ticket seller.

Finally the old woman moved off, heading for booth six. A moment later the arrow flashed for booth nine. Sebastian hurried over.

Behind a glass barrier, a bored looking man sat, staring at a screen just off to Sebastian's left.

"Where to?" the man said.

"Next train to London," Sebastian said.

"The next train leaves at thirteen thirty hours," the man said. He punched into a keyboard in front of him. "That will be..."

"Nothing," Sebastian said.

"What?" Puzzled, the man glanced over. Sebastian captured his gaze.

"It will be nothing," Sebastian said. "You will print the ticket and delete the transaction from your system. You haven't sold a ticket to London now."

A Remembrance of Flesh

The man's lips moved. The muscles in his cheeks twitched. This was a far bigger Influence than Sebastian had done with the people in line and took all of his remaining reserves. He could feel his body sweating. His heart started pounding, sending adrenaline through his system to combat the stress of his concentration. His breath came shallow although he tried to take deeper breaths. His body seemed unable to relax, more sweat staining his underarms and trickling down his legs. He could feel his hands trembling at his sides. He clenched them into fists, pressing them against his thighs. The pounding in his temples spread across his forehead, sending pain piercing into his eyes. The man in front of him seemed to tremble then jerked to face his screen. His hands spasmed on the keyboard then shot out to grab the printed ticket.

He shoved it through the slot. Sebastian grabbed it and retreated. As he backed away, the man's agitation lessened. He sagged in his chair, head tilting toward the screen. As soon as he was no longer looking his way, Sebastian turned and stumbled away.

The pounding in his head lessened. His heart rate slowed, allowing him to take deeper, slower breathes that in turn slowed his heart beat even more. All his muscles trembled and he felt like he wanted to sink to the floor. Instead he stumbled to a bench set in a corner by a coffee kiosk.

He finally looked at the ticket.

Only half an hour. He wanted to rest for a moment but he could already feel his body sagging against the bench. If he waited any longer he wouldn't be able to stand up again soon. Better just get to the train.

He forced himself to stand and move. By the time he reached the gate, the train was already boarding. Now or never. Would he be able to stand it on the train or should he try to find other transportation? He was already here and the fatigue he felt actually deadened his desire for blood. A train trip of a few hours might actually help. Maybe he could sleep and avoid contact with everyone.

With that hope, he clutched the ticket and boarded the train to London.

His last thought as he stepped on board was wondering if Jessica was okay.

He slept most of the way and woke groggy when the train arrived in London. He stumbled through the station and out into the street filled with people and traffic. Sounds and smells assaulted him. After the relative comfort on the train because he'd slept, the sudden assault overwhelmed him. The urge to lash out at everyone who walked by increased with every person around him. He pushed through the crowd.

There, a corner.

He hurried forward and raced around it. A side street. Fewer people, fewer cars. He almost ran as he kept turning corners, getting farther and farther from a main street.

Finally he ended up on a residential street. Quiet. One car drove by, tires hissing on the pavement. No one walked the sidewalks.

He was alone and he could breathe.

His entire body sagged with relief. It had been so long since he'd spent any real length of time with regular people. It was overwhelming. Would he be more used to it if he hadn't spent so much time around the In-Between this past year? Impossible to say. For now, he just had to be aware of his own weakness and stay away from people.

Unfortunately that posed a problem now because he needed to eat something. He could feel the need in his body. All the activity, running from the vampires, the In-Between, even dealing with the pull of the book, had sapped his energy. His last meal in the bar with Jessica seemed a long time ago or maybe he'd just burned through it.

Were they feeding her now, taking care of her? She was much more their kind than he ever was but she'd rejected them to come with him. He knew they'd punish her for it, he just didn't know how much. He wanted to find her, help her, but knew he couldn't, not and leave the book out here for the vampires to find. Odds were Constantine was getting close and Kobol wouldn't be far behind. Sebastian hadn't met any of the other clan heads but he could imagine they were searching as well.

Did Stan have any idea of the nightmares heading his way?

Food. If he had any chance of getting to the book first, he would need all his energy. Although it was late afternoon it might be early enough to find an unoccupied house. He sent out psychic feelers, searching as he walked along. The energy from the people stood out in his mind, making it easier to pass them by. Finally he came to a small red brick house, squished between two larger grey ones. It held an emptiness to it, empty all day from the feel.

He took a casual look around. No one in sight. He strolled up to the front door, pulling out his small lock pick as if it was a key. Shielding his hands with his body, he worked the pick into the lock. It took a moment, just... wait... another turn and there, the lock clicked and he turned the door knob. The door opened and he entered.

In the quietness of the front hall, he paused after closing the door. Still the feeling of emptiness although he did feel some indication of life. He moved quietly into the living room and found an aquarium full of bright fish. The air cleaner hummed and bubbles rotated in a cycle up to the surface.

He smiled at the fish and went into the kitchen. It was small, painted a lime green with dark green cupboards. He pulled out the fixings for a sandwich and made himself two ham and cheese on rye bread. He didn't want to intrude more than necessary and since nothing had any flavor anyway, it didn't make any sense to bother with actual cooking.

He ate standing over the sink, letting any crumbles fall as he leaned over. Sure enough, even the addition of mustard and some cayenne pepper added nothing to the taste for him. He just chewed and swallowed, chewed and swallowed. A mechanical motion designed to feed his body. He took no pleasure in it but at least he could tell it helped with his energy level.

By the time he'd finished both sandwiches, he felt better, stronger and more able to deal with any people out there. He washed the knife he'd used and put it away. He made sure everything in the fridge looked the same then he wiped down the counter and washed the crumbs down the drain.

As he shut off the water tap, silence pressed in on him, making him sleepy. Maybe he could lie down for a few minutes. The sleep on the train hadn't been all that restful, not with the jostling and trying to get comfortable while sitting upright.

Just a few minutes.

He found a small bedroom upstairs that had the generic look of a guest room. Simple double bed with a burgundy blanket. Bland paintings of flowers decorated the pink walls. A single dresser sat between the door and a small closet, empty except for a single white doily. He lay down on top of the covers. He left his shoes on but hung his feet over the end of the bed. He didn't want to have to worry about putting them back on. The thought drifted away as his eyes closed.

He found himself again in the house decorated in remnants of his childhood. It didn't seem at all strange to see the floral couch his mother had tossed when he was seven sitting on the new rug they had bought just before he'd left for college. In a way they matched very well, the pale pink of the carpeting matching the paleness of the some of the flowers in the couch. Too bad his mother had gotten rid of it, but Callum had thrown up on the cushions one too many times. He kept making such a fuss over the blood, he wouldn't even take it from the bottle. He just left people strewn all over the floor and Sebastian had to clean it up.

It wasn't even his mess!

"Clean up every drop." Kobol stood in the doorway of the living room. His hands were on his hips. A blue cape flowed off his shoulders like a superhero's cape.

"Don't miss anything."

"I'm getting it," Sebastian said. He picked up the papers from the coffee table and began dabbing at the stain on the cushion.

"And don't spill on yourself," said Kobol.

"I won't!" Sebastian rolled his eyes and grabbed another piece of paper. Strange squiggles and diagrams covered the page. He crumpled it and wiped the cushion.

"You always spill on yourself." Jessica stood by the window. She pulled her hair back from her face and tied it back in a pony tail.

"Not always."

"Often enough." She slung her backpack over her shoulder and slid it onto her back. "Just make sure you don't spill anything onto the book."

"I won't."

"I mean it." She wagged her finger at him. "Don't you dare spill a drop. Not a single drop. Got that?" She clenched her teeth at him and he saw the fangs protruding down.

"I got it. I won't spill a drop. Can't you let me finish here?"

He turned away from her to grab another piece of paper and finish moping up this stain. Boy, his brother Callum sure had a lot of blood in him.

Fingers closed on his biceps and squeezed, pulling on him. He turned to find Jessica staring right in his face. Her fangs were gone. Her face was pale and drawn. Her clothing looked rumpled and weathered. Her backpack had vanished.

"Are you hearing me, Sebastian?" she said. "You have to listen, you have to hear what I'm telling you."

"I got it," he said. "I won't spill a drop."

"No," she said. "That's not it. You have to spill it all, all over the book. That's the only way to destroy it. Spill it all, make sure you spill it all!"

She screamed.

He jolted away. A woman stood in the doorway of the small bedroom. She held her hand to her chest. Shock stretched her thin features. Then she jumped back and slammed the door shut.

Shit, Sebastian thought. He leapt out of bed and scooped up the backpack lying by the bed. How long had he been asleep? Way too long.

"Denis!" He heard the woman shouting downstairs. "There's a man in the spare bedroom!"

Time to go.

He opened the door and peered out. Only one set of stairs heading down. He didn't really feel like meeting up with Denis on the way down. He closed the door and moved to the window. What was it with windows for him? Why was he always having to climb out of windows?

When he looked out, he saw an old tree only a couple of feet from the window. A large branch curved toward and then angled away. He should be able to make it.

He slid the window open and unhooked the screen, pulling it in to lean it on the wall beside the window. As he hitched the backpack onto his shoulders, he heard stomping from the stairs.

No time to lose.

He climbed out onto the window ledge, a bare three inches wide. Look across, not down. Don't look down. Look at the tree. It's just over there. Barely a step across. Hanging onto the window frame, he bent his legs. A good solid push off and he'd make it easy.

Behind him, the door slammed open. A man yelled.

Sebastian leapt into the air.

His arms grabbed the branch. His right hand slipped but his left arm hung on, long enough for him to grab again with his right hand. With both hands secure, he inched closer to the tree until he felt it against his body. Then he let go of the branch, to grab smaller branches and start to climb down.

A man appeared in the window on the second floor.

"Come back here!"

Not likely. Sebastian increased his pace and when he was a few feet from the ground, he dropped, landing with bended knees. His hands smacked the ground, bracing himself.

No time to linger. He stood up and started running down the street, grateful to find that while he'd been asleep the sun had gone down, leaving the street bathed in darkness, broken only by the occasional street light.

He ducked down the next street, then took another right and another left. Soon he couldn't even remember which way he'd come. Certainly Denis wasn't going to be able to catch him.

He paused at the corner, under the sagging branches of a willow tree. His heart thudded in his chest as he gulped in air. Around him he heard the night sounds of the neighborhood. Crickets chirped in the grass. A breeze rustled the branches around him, creating a hiss in the air. A few streets over he heard car engines. A baby cried two doors down across the street. As usual in the night his senses came fully alive and he heard everything.

Or so he thought until the hand reached from behind him and grabbed him by the throat.

CHAPTER THIRTEEN

Sebastian choked as the hand tightened, cutting off his air.

"Tell me why I shouldn't snap your neck right now." The voice purred in his ear. A sour stench enveloped him. Vampire smell. He recognized that voice.

Leon.

He grabbed at the fingers but they tightened even more, digging into his neck. Sebastian felt his windpipe close. His mouth gaped open as he gasped for air but with the hand tightening and tightening, he couldn't draw a breath. How odd, he thought, that it would be difficult to draw in something as small as oxygen. No one could see those molecules with a naked eye and yet by closing his throat, he couldn't draw them in. Maybe those bright silver flashes starting to burst in front of his eyes were oxygen molecules...

The hand released.

Sebastian crashed to the ground. His throat opened and he sucked in air, making a loud groaning sound. Glorious air rushed into his lungs. His body sagged on the ground. He didn't think he was ever more grateful for the simple act of breathing.

A foot stomped down on the sidewalk in front of his face. He looked up to see Leon looming over him. Fury etched itself into that young face, giving it an aged countenance. Now Sebastian could see the weight of years, of decades, hanging on the boy. No, not a boy, far older than Sebastian so he couldn't even be called a man but was simply vampire. The sour, rotting, death-filled existence of a vampire.

"Why?" Sebastian tested his voice. It came out in a croak. "Why not kill me?"

Leon crouched until his face was close to Sebastian's. The sour stench almost made Sebastian gag.

"I want the book," Leon said. "You can find it. Kobol was right. You're the only one who can find it for sure and you're going to find it for me or I'll strip the flesh from your bones and then I'll do it to her."

He meant Jessica, Sebastian knew. It didn't matter that she was surrounded by In-Between, one day she wouldn't be and Leon would get to her. It didn't matter how long it took. A vampire could afford the patience of years, of decades.

"All right," Sebastian said. "I'll find the book."

Leon reached down. One clawed hand gripped Sebastian's shirt and yanked him to his feet. He pushed Sebastian forward. Sebastian stumbled and righted himself, starting to walk down the sidewalk.

"How did you find me?" he said.

"I am an expert tracker, even among vampires," Leon said. "I have your scent and the girl's. I could follow you to the ends of the earth." He smirked. "You didn't even try to hide your scent."

They walked in silence for a few minutes. After he destroyed the book, he was going to have to kill Leon, Sebastian knew. If the vampire was really that good a tracker he would never stop hunting them. He would have to die.

Assuming Sebastian could find the book and destroy it.

Easy, right?

Sure it was.

"Where are we going?" Sebastian said.

"Find the book," Leon said. "You tell me where it is." He grabbed Sebastian's arm and yanked him to a stop. "Find it now."

His claws dug in to Sebastian's arm. Sebastian shook it off. "I can't focus with you grabbing me."

Leon glared. "Find it."

"Okay, okay." Sebastian closed his eyes. He took a deep breath and let it out. As soon as he thought of the book the background itch that had buried itself in the back of his mind rose to the surface. He could feel the calling of the book. It tugged at him, a seductive pull promising so much power. He could easily take care of this pathetic creature in front of him and any one else who tried to stand against him or threatened someone he loved. All he had to do was follow...

His eyes opened and he turned to the right. He moved forward. Footsteps eating up the sidewalk. Leon had to hurry to catch up.

"Which way?" Leon said.

"Shut up and follow," Sebastian said.

He heard the vampire growl beside him but he ignored it. Instead he focused on the call in his mind, the itch that propelled him forward. His feet stumbled over each other as he hurried forward. The streets became a blur of color and images. Store fronts and people surged by. He could feel himself hurrying along, sometimes running, sometimes walking fast, always with the whisper of the book in his head.

Come forward, come find me.

He would find it.

The surroundings blurred around him. He heard his voice murmuring but didn't know what he was saying, or if he was even saying it. It didn't feel like they were his words, but something else talking through him. The book, he realized, as he got closer to it, it came through more clearly, taking more control. Would he be able to wrestle control back?

Would he be able to destroy it?

Pain laced through his head as he thought it. He stumbled on tile, for a moment noticing his surroundings. A subway station. He was underground. Then the pain asserted itself again.

The book didn't like him thinking about its destruction.

He buried the thought in the back of his head. *Where are you? Show me where you are.*

The familiar tingling started again and he moved on.

When he came back to himself again, he was outside in the street. Darkness filled the area. Even the street lights seemed distant. Large quiet buildings stood around him. They had an air of the industrial to them. He smelled moisture in the air.

Stumbling footsteps sounded behind him. He turned to see Leon standing a little farther down the street. He leaned over, resting his hands on his knees. He looked like he was breathing heavily. Did vampires need to breathe?

Leon straightened and moved forward, his gate a little slower but still moving with that smooth, gliding grace.

"Don't go running again," he said. "I'll find you no matter where you go."

"I wasn't running," Sebastian said.

"Yes, you were. You ran all the way here from the subway station." Leon tilted his head. "Why aren't you tired?"

Subway station? Sebastian didn't remember it. He didn't remember the subway or even heading down the stairs. He had a vague recollection of tiles but nothing more came to mind. He shivered. Had the book taken over? Maybe this was a mistake, maybe he should have insisted he and Jessica run as far as possible to get away from it. But even as he thought it, he knew it wouldn't have worked. No matter where he was he would have felt the book, now that it had awoken.

The flesh remembered.

"It's close," he said. He turned away from Leon and headed up the street. The scent of moisture grew stronger. He heard the light lapping of water. They must be near the river.

His footsteps echoed in the air then he realized it wasn't an echo. Someone was trailing along. Over to the left, by the dark building next to an alley, he thought he saw a glimpse of fabric...

A snarl broke the night. Figures burst from the shadows, racing forward, impossibly fast. Vampires! Sebastian started running, dodging grasping claws, leaping over bodies that flung themselves in his path. Shrieks sounded behind him, followed by snarls. The sound of bodies slamming into each other punctuated the yells. He risked one glance over his shoulder as he ran.

Leon was surrounded by vampires. They fell on him, ripping and tearing. Fabric and hunks of flesh flew into the air. Would they kill him?

He'd never heard of vampires killing their own. Then he caught a glimpse of a pixie haircut, wisps angling along a familiar cheekbone.

Alexa...

He ran.

Constantine's clan. They would be coming after him as soon as they dispatched Leon.

His heart hammered in his chest. His feet pounded the asphalt. The backpack jostled up and down on his back, the straps digging into his shoulders. He wished he could rip it off and leave it behind. Maybe Frank's papers would distract them for a moment but even if he could afford the energy to yank the backpack from his shoulders, he couldn't do that to Jessica. Those papers were the last piece of her friend. That was more important to him than he'd realized before.

Just when was he going to really accept that he loved her?

Not really the proper time for this but he might not have any other time. He wished he'd told her rather than danced around it. Dammit, he seemed destined to regret his inability to say what he felt for his whole life.

However short that ended up being.

He reached a corner and turned left. The street narrowed, smaller buildings pressing against the sidewalks. Now he thought he heard steps behind him. The vampires giving chase. Would they hold back to have some sport with him or would they come fast to finish him off for good?

There was a silver knife in the backpack but he'd never have a chance to pull it out now.

Keep running.

In the distance, he saw a spire just to the left. A church. Holy water. At least it would be something he could use in a fight. He pumped his arms, adding a burst of speed. His thighs ached. His chest hurt. His lungs felt like they were burning. He tried to suck in air through his nose. His mouth was parched. Ahead half a block he caught sight of the white pavement in front of the church. He angled to the left.

Footsteps coming from behind him. Could he reach the church? He dared one glance back. Figures raced forward, still some distance away in the dark. They appeared to be running flat out. Why hadn't they caught him? He didn't understand.

He reached the church grounds and leapt up the steps three at a time. Just before he slammed into the door he wondered what he'd do if the door was locked. *Die*, came the thought floating up from the back of his mind.

Very true.

He grabbed the thick brass handle and yanked, half expecting to experience the resistance of a lock. The door swung open. He ducked inside.

Lock the door.

His hands fumbled over the door's surface. He found a lock and twisted it. Then he reached to the top of the door and the bottom, feeling for the small bolts that gave an extra lock. Both bolts flipped up. He backed away from the door. A moment later, something slammed into it. The heavy wood groaned but held. He heard snarls of anger outside.

How long before they broke through the windows?

Moments.

He entered the main body of the church. Two large bowls of water sat on either side of the door. He yanked the backpack from his shoulders and unzipped it. If he had a bottle he could fill it with holy water.

Nothing.

He closed it and shoved it back onto his shoulders. Maybe coming into this church wasn't such a good idea...

"Who's there?"

The soft voice came from the right, deeper in the shadows. Sebastian looked over and saw a man crouching under the low overhanging balcony. Something about his long stringy hair looked familiar.

"Stan?"

The man's hands fluttered up in panic. He started backing away.

"Wait! I'm Sebastian. Remember me? I was a friend of Charlie's. We came to see you one night, about the In-Between."

"You! Fuck!" He spun around and pushed through a curtain hanging in front of the wall.

Sebastian ran forward. He grabbed the curtain and yanked. A small narrow door. He grabbed the handle. Locked. He began pulling on it, twisting. It wasn't strong. A good yank and he'd be able to pull it off the hinges.

"Wait, wait!" Stan's voice sounded muffled behind the wood. Sebastian heard the slide of a bolt and he pulled the door open.

"Just lock it, damn you," Stan said.

Sebastian entered and closed the door behind him. He slid the bolt home. This door wasn't going to hold the vampires for long. He turned to face total darkness. One blink and his In-Between senses kicked in. His vision processed total darkness in shades of grey. He saw narrow stairs heading downward. Stan already huddled at the bottom.

Sebastian headed down. Stan's face turned toward him although Sebastian knew he had to be blind in this darkness.

"Stan, it's me," Sebastian said.

"Of course it is," Stan said. "It was always you, wasn't it? Charlie died because of you, I learned about the In-Between and the vampires because of you."

"Charlie?" Sebastian said. "How did you know about him?"

"A wild animal? Who could believe that story? I watched people I knew pretend it was true. Over time they just forgot about it, about him, but I couldn't. I remembered all of you coming over that night and the crazy stuff Charlie had asked me to look up. So I hacked into the school computer and found that Alexa Hammond had disappeared and you had left school. Did she get killed too?"

"Yes," Sebastian said. "Well, she got turned into a vampire."

"Shit."

"Yeah. Listen, is there another way out? Those vampires will be able to get through that door in no time."

Stan frowned at Sebastian's left shoulder. "I thought vampires couldn't come into a church."

"A lot of that stuff doesn't apply," Sebastian said.

Stan turned away. He knelt on the floor, his hands fumbling around. After a moment, he stood up. Light sprang from the flashlight in his hands, exposing a narrow tunnel that led off to the right. Sebastian blinked. His eyes adjusted to the flare of light.

"This way." Stan began to hurry along the tunnel. The light bobbed in his hand, revealing the rough stone of the walls and ceiling. A dirt floor was beneath their feet as they ran. The acoustics of the tunnel were strange. The sound of the vampires at the door faded behind them sooner than Sebastian expected. He imagined he'd be hearing them again soon enough once they got through the door and down the narrow stairway.

Stan ran full out ahead of him and Sebastian hurried to keep up. The light zig zagged in crazy patterns around the walls. Sebastian thought he saw streaks of red on the yellowish brick but each time he tried to look, Stan sped off causing Sebastian to rush to catch up. The only thing he could smell was dust from the floor and bricks and the foul stench of Stan's fear.

The tunnel turned left and angled downward in a slow slope. Stan scraped his arm against the brick as he turned the corner. That must be what made the red marks, Sebastian thought. He managed to slow enough to take the turn without hitting the wall.

As the tunnel levelled off, it headed into a straight away. How far down had they gone? Sebastian couldn't tell. They'd been running at full speed for over fifteen minutes. Strange, the vampires should have broken through the door from the church by now. They would have headed straight down the stairs and followed them into the tunnel. He should at least hear them growling or running in the distance.

But he didn't hear anything except for Stan's ragged breath.

The acoustics maybe? A nagging doubt niggled at him.

"Where are we going?" he yelled.

"Another way out!" Stan yelled back over his shoulder. The light jumped, illuminating a door in the distance. It was the first thing that looked like a barrier that Sebastian had seen in this tunnel.

A door, thank god.

When they reached it, Sebastian noticed how old it looked. A heavy oak door with strips of steel welded across it. The lock was huge and Stan pulled out what looked like an old skeleton key to open it. He jiggled the key and tugged at the handle. Nothing. He shifted and the flashlight he'd held under his arm slipped to the ground.

"I'll hold it." Sebastian scooped it up and angled the beam down on the lock. Stan jiggled the key again, trying to get it to turn more but the handle still wouldn't move. Sebastian glanced down the tunnel. Shouldn't he be hearing the vampires by now?

Something felt very odd.

He started to inch back down the tunnel, keeping the flashlight beam pointed at Stan's hands. Maybe if Sebastian just returned to that first turn and took a look...

"Got it!"

The handle clicked. Sebastian turned to see Stan lifting the handle and pushing the door open. It moved slowly, scraping across a stone floor. As Sebastian followed Stan through he saw that the door was almost six inches thick. With more scraping on the floor, Sebastian shoved the door shut. He turned to find Stan returning with a large wooden beam that fit across the door, resting in two latches on either side.

Sebastian's shoulders drooped. No vampire would be coming through that door. Not without hours of effort. Hell, considering how thick that door was, maybe not in several nights of effort.

Sebastian turned away from the door to face the inner chamber. The entrance led several steps down into the main area, a large circular room, almost fifty feet in diameter. Stan moved down the stairs to a large wooden table in the center of the room. On it, he lit four lanterns and started spacing them around the room. Even with them turned to their highest setting, they did little to dispel all the shadows that lurked around the room. Sebastian looked up and saw the ceiling sloped up, disappearing into darkness. A blink of his eyes and his vision adjusted for him to make out the dome rising high about their heads.

Something about that ceiling. He squinted, trying to focus upward. With the darkness he couldn't be sure. Was something engraved in the ceiling?

"Want a drink?" Stan said.

Sebastian started. Stan lifted a bottle and wagged the neck at him.

"It's good stuff," he said.

"No, not for me," Sebastian said.

Stan shrugged. He splashed some into two glasses and slid the second glass in Sebastian's direction. "In case you change your mind."

"Thanks," Sebastian said.

Stan downed his drink then poured himself another. He downed the second one as fast as the first. Sebastian wondered how long he'd keep doing that but after the second one, Stan replaced the cap on the bottle. He grabbed one of the chairs sitting against the wall and dragged it to the table. He collapsed into it. His head rested in his hands.

"What a mess. What a goddamn mess."

"No kidding," Sebastian said. He noticed another chair sitting beside the door. He went to get it and brought it back to the table.

Stan pulled his third drink over and sipped at it. "At least a toast to Charlie?" he said.

A sudden pang of guilt almost made Sebastian double over. "Sure," he said. "To Charlie."

"To Charlie." Stan raised his glass. Sebastian touched his glass to Stan's. They drank.

"It's been a goddamn mess since he asked me to look into those In-Between," Stan said. "How am I supposed to live with something like this after he's killed, knowing what I know? I knew some motherfucker vampire killed him. I knew those In-Between were trying to kill them. When I couldn't find you, I went looking for them."

Stan pulled the bottle close again and unscrewed the lid. He splashed more into his glass.

"It took about six months to get them to trust me," he said. "They were trying to get that book for ages before I came along. I helped them build a viable model so they could figure out how to get in. Worked like a charm, or should have, but some of the vampires escaped." Stan sucked back his drink. "They were supposed to bring the book right to me but instead they took it to Corbin. Just because they fucking trusted him more."

"They wanted him to translate it," Sebastian said.

"I could have done that," Stan said. "I've got translation programs all ready to go. I input everything into them. Every arcane thing I could find. It would have worked perfectly. I finally convinced Corbin of that."

"He gave you the book," Sebastian said.

Stan nodded. "He had to. When he realized the vampires were after him, he didn't have any choice. Nowhere else was safe. I made sure of that."

He splashed more whisky into his glass and drank it. He slammed the glass down on the table.

"What?" Sebastian said.

"You heard me," Stan said.

He pulled out a gun and shot Sebastian.

CHAPTER FOURTEEN

Sebastian felt the dart slammed into the left pectoral muscle in his chest. The impact knocked him back in his chair. The chair rocked on its legs, teetered, then spilled Sebastian onto the floor. He tried to put his hands out to catch himself but his muscles wouldn't work. His body wasn't responding to his commands. He fell on his side, his face slapping the floor. He felt his inner cheek scrap against his teeth. Blood trickled into his mouth and out his lips onto the floor.

The last thing he saw before he lost consciousness was Stan's dusty running shoes approaching...

"How long before he wakes up?" A male voice growled.

"Should be soon."

Stan's voice. Sebastian recognized it.

"It had better be." The male voice again and this time Sebastian recognized it as well. He'd only heard it a couple of times before but he remembered. Oh yes, he remembered it.

Constantine.

Stan had betrayed him to Constantine. Why? Had this been Stan's game all along when he started connecting with the In-Between?

He wanted to ask but doubted they'd be in a chatty mood. As he became more aware of his own body, he realized he was still lying on his side, the cold floor pressing on his cheek. His hands were tied behind his back. His ankles bent in painfully as well, indicating they were tied too.

"His breathing has changed. I can hear it from here."

A woman's voice. A voice he'd known for years, one he'd loved before he'd lost her to Constantine.

Alexa.

"Trying to play possum, boy?" Constantine said. His voice was now right above Sebastian. "We can't have that."

A hand dug into Sebastian's arm and yanked him up off the floor. He hung with his legs dragging as Constantine lifted him. His claws tightened around Sebastian's bicep, pinching the skin. He dragged Sebastian to a chair and dumped him into it.

"We know you're awake," Constantine said. "Don't make me rip off your eyelids."

Sebastian opened his eyes.

"Hello, sleeping beauty."

Constantine's lips twisted into a wry smile. A black beard framed his lips and black hair curled down his head to his shoulders. The paleness of his skin accentuated the blackness of his hair.

"Can't we just get on with it?" Stan said. He leaned his butt against a wooden crate by the wall. His arms crossed against his narrow chest. His shoulders hunched. From the expression on his face, Sebastian guessed the man wasn't too happy with how things were progressing.

But Stan didn't hold his attention for long. Movement to the right caught his eye. Sebastian turned.

Alexa stepped from the shadows into the light from the lantern.

The paleness of her skin surprised him. He'd always remembered her with her olive complexion, so perfect with her brown hair. Now the warm olive color had blanched from her skin just as the life had been leached from her eyes. They were the same eyes that looked at him, the same deep brown behind her glasses but now he saw how lifeless, how soulless they were. They were the eyes of the vampire who had jumped on Charlie and tore his throat out. They weren't the eyes of the woman Sebastian had loved.

Who he had still loved for a time, but now looking at her again, with that pale skin and even as her lips twisted in a smile that matched the one he was so familiar with, he really knew she was gone. And his love for her was only a memory. A regret he'd never spoken about.

"He almost smells like us," Alexa said.

"Yes," Constantine said. "He's very close. That's why he's so perfect. None of the other In-Between got this close without turning or dying. That's what makes this such a unique opportunity, and we wouldn't have had that without your help, Stan."

"Right," Stan said. "So you keep saying. I've done my part. I got the book out of the vampire library like you wanted. I got it away from the In-Between and now you've got Sebastian. So when do I get turned?"

"You want to be a vampire?" Sebastian said. "Are you nuts?"

Stan pushed off from the crate and stormed over. "I'm not nuts. My dad died of cancer when I was a kid. He was forty-two. My mom got breast cancer when I was in my teens. It's all over my family. Uncles with brain tumors, cousins with lung cancer. I'm twenty-four wondering if I'll see my thirty-fifth birthday. I won't die like that."

"So you'll kill other people and drink their blood," Sebastian said.

"I don't have to kill people to survive," Stan said. "I won't need a person's full blood to live. I just need to take a little. Like a pint or so a night. No big deal."

"Is that what he tells you?" Sebastian nodded his head at Constantine who smiled.

"I've told him the truth," Constantine said. "A vampire can survive on as little as a pint a night. As much as a simple blood donation."

"Sure," Sebastian said. "Because you do that all the time. You hardly ever gorge yourself on people, drink every last drop and leave them crumpled on the floor. Or turn them into another soulless freak like you."

Constantine swatted him across the face as if he was swatting a fly. Sebastian's head rocked back. He felt the tear in his cheek open again. He tasted blood and felt it dribble down his chin.

Both Constantine and Alexa perked up with interest but neither moved to take advantage of his blood flow. As an In-Between he was poison to them, to any vampire other than the one who had tried to turn him. They knew better than to drink him.

He glanced over at Stan and saw a frown of uncertainness on his face.

"Or maybe they won't turn you all the way and you'll end up like me. In-Between. But you think the other In-Between will help you after what you've done?"

"I don't have any choice," Stan said. He pressed his hands together by his waist, the knuckles whitening from pressure.

"Sure, keep telling yourself that," Sebastian said.

"That's enough." Constantine turned his back on Sebastian and crossed the room to Stan. "I want the book now. It's time to complete the ritual."

"Ritual?" Sebastian said.

Constantine turned and raised a finger to his lips. "Hush now. I'll gag you if I must."

Sebastian pressed his lips together. He wanted to know about the ritual. He had a feeling he wasn't going to like it.

Spill it all, make sure you spill it all.

The phrase jolted him. Where had that come from? The image of his mother's floral couch floated through his mind. He remembered a vague dream. Something about spilling on the couch...

Spilling on the book.

Spill it all...

Jessica's voice, the voice of safety, the voice he trusted. Was that what they were going to do to him? Spill all of his blood on the book? What would that do?

He was afraid to find out. But maybe if they spilled all his blood he wouldn't be alive to know it.

Somehow that wasn't comforting either.

"The book, Stan, I need the book now," Constantine said.

"What about our deal?" Stan said. "I've done everything you asked. When are you going to turn me?"

"When the ritual is completed," Constantine said. "I'll be that much more powerful. That power will be shared with you. You will be able to become a clan head on your own, loyal to me, once the others have been enslaved."

"I don't want to be a clan head. I just want to live forever."

"You say that now." Constantine draped an arm across Stan's narrow shoulders. "But eternal life without power is boring and weak. You would be forced to serve others, or even me. This way, you will be on top. You will be the one in control. You will command others."

A twinkling of interest lit in Stan's eye. "Really?"

"Of course. I won't be able to deal with everything. I will need to delegate."

"He's lying," Sebastian said. "Can't you see that? He'll kill you once you hand over the book."

Constantine flicked a finger in Alexa's direction. She crossed to stand behind Sebastian. She grabbed his jaw and forced it open. He tried to turn his head away but her grip was like iron. She stuffed a gag into his mouth and tied it in place.

Stan frowned at the sight of Sebastian struggling in the chair. "Was that necessary?"

"Never mind him," Constantine said. "He's In-Between. You know yourself how they are, unstable, caught between human and vampire. They never had the chance to turn fully and they're angry about it. They had the opportunity for immortality but it was stolen from them. He will die just like you will, if you stay as you are."

Constantine pointed a finger at Stan's chest. "But we aren't going to let that happen, are we?"

"No," Stan said.

Constantine smiled. "Of course not. Where is the book?"

"You couldn't change me and then give me power after?" Stan said.

Constantine shook his head. "It doesn't work that way. I change you now and you will be subservient to me always. Only after I have the power from the book will I be able to share it with you."

Stan's shoulders drooped. "Okay." He turned away from Constantine and crossed the room to an area of dark shadows. Sebastian adjusted his vision and noticed the second door for the first time. He took a quick look around the room and saw four other doors set deep in the walls in pockets of shadows. They all had the same heavy wood look with the steel reinforcements. Where did these doors lead to? Who had made this room?

He glanced up again to the domed ceiling and the familiar looking scratches on the stone. He knew he'd never seen them before but the feeling of familiarity was so strong. Dizziness began to spin in his head. He felt as if all the blood in his body was draining from his head to his feet. His hands felt limp in the rope. The rope loosened around his wrists and even drooped at his ankles. He stared at the scratches. Were they figures or arcane letters? Commands or invocations? His body relaxed deeper in the chair. His muscles felt as loose as putty. The ropes loosened farther.

His hands twisted a little, just an inch or so. One loop of rope drooped down the back of his hand. It felt slick with sweat. His heart started to pound. His muscles started to tighten. Relax... Look at the scratches... Look at the dome... He stared upward. His body relaxed again, the muscles released.

The rope slipped farther, then farther again. Now it hung near the knuckles on his right hand. Another inch or so and he could pull his hand free. No, not pull, just slip it free with the slightest movement. He focused on his ankles and felt the rope drooping there, loosening. He wiggled his feet, his toes. The rope loosened...

At his hands, the rope dropped past his fingernails. His right hand came free. He grabbed the length of rope as it slid away, stopping it from falling to the floor. He tilted his head back down. Only seconds had passed. Stan still stood at the door. He gave a tug and the door swung open, scraping against the hard stone floor.

Sebastian dropped his gaze to the table and let it travel down beneath it. He saw the shape of his backpack under the table, leaning against one wooden leg. In the drink holder, the top of a small knife handle protruded. The bigger silver blade was zipped inside the backpack but he'd never be able to get to it. The smaller silver paring knife would have to do.

Spill it all...

Now he just had to wait, wait for the book, wait for Constantine to get close.

Just wait.

Stan returned, carrying a plastic bag. He left the door open as he stepped back into the room. As he began to cross to Constantine, pounding sounded on two of the other doors. Stan jumped and clutched the plastic bag.

"What's that?"

Constantine scented the air and nodded to Alexa. "Some of my clan, returning from patrol." He crossed to one of the doors as Alexa crossed to the one opposite.

"Wait a minute, I only said it could be you two," Stan said. "I don't want a gang of vampires in here."

"That's not very polite, Stan. They have come to see my ascension. Would you deny them when they will soon be your brothers?" Constantine unlocked the door and yanked it open.

Three vampires slipped inside before the door fully opened. They looked dishevelled. Another two entered from Alexa's door, covered in dust. One had ripped jeans and limped.

"What's going on?" Constantine said.

"In-Between," said the vampire closest to him. "I don't know how. We dispatched Kobol's toady and they fell on us almost immediately. We weren't prepared."

"Meaning you were sloppy," Constantine said.

"They came in fast, in numbers," the vampire said. "We didn't know what was happening."

Constantine growled and turned toward Sebastian. "You led them here!"

"Hmm?" Sebastian said around the gag. He tried to project his innocence. How would he know the In-Between were following him. Unless...

Oh Jessica, what sly lie did you tell?

Constantine scowled. "Give me the book." He held out his hand to Stan.

Stan clutched the bag and took a step back, aiming for the open door behind him. Sebastian shook his head and tried to signal him. Too late. Stan took one more step and bumped into Alexa. Her hands wrenched the bag from his arms and she tossed it to Constantine. Stan whimpered as she shoved him away. He tripped and sprawled on the floor.

"Hey, that wasn't necessary," he said.

"Shut up," she said, "or I'll rip out your throat myself."

Stan's mouth snapped shut. He hugged his knees to his chest.

Constantine crossed to the table and pulled the book from the plastic bag. He tossed the bag behind him and set the book down on the table top. He took a deep breath and then opened the book with reverence.

From across the table, Sebastian could see the pages, thin and delicate. The color was a dull brown, like the color of tea soaking into the pages, but he knew it wasn't tea. Even from here he could see the dried brown scribbles, scratched by a sharpened quill dipped into a bowl of blood. Sebastian felt his body quiver as he looked at the book. He could almost smell the foulness, the decay that emanated from it.

But it made Constantine smile.

The vampire turned the pages with increasing speed. He nodded to himself. "It's here, can you feel it, Alexa? The power is here to enslave all the clan heads, to make them do my will. And you'll have your part to play, boy."

Constantine slid the book along the table as he walked around toward Sebastian. His free hand flexed, revealing claws. He held the book open on the table and lifted his arm.

"Alha grenko Grellock abasio dalecan freeyho!"

The arm began to swing. Sebastian dove under the table. His hands came free from the loose rope. He grabbed the small knife and rolled. Constantine dropped to his knees and reached for Sebastian. Sebastian kicked out. Constantine grabbed one foot and dragged him out from under the table. He whipped his arm up, flipping Sebastian up onto the table like a huge side of beef. Sebastian landed on his side. His breath whooshed out of him. His limbs flailed but he managed to hold onto the small knife.

Constantine's hand wrapped around Sebastian's throat, pinning him to the table. He moved the book a little closer and turned a page.

"Abasio dalecan freeyho trebla macio..."

Sebastian swung with the knife. He slashed the hand holding his throat. Constantine howled and pulled his hand away. Sebastian sat up. He grabbed the book and thrust it at Constantine. Reflexively, the vampire took the book, pressing it into his chest. Sebastian swung the blade and sliced open Constantine's throat. Blood sprayed out, splashing the floor and soaking the book in Constantine's arms. The vampire's eyes widened. He dropped to his knees.

Spill it all...

Sebastian backhanded with the knife. It caught Constantine across the face. His cheek opened. More blood spilled. It poured down the front of his body, over the book.

From the other side of the table, Sebastian heard a shriek. Alexa ran forward and vaulted over the table. Her hands reached out for him, claws extending. The other vampires moved when she did, surrounding him and Constantine. Howling, snarling.

Before her hands reached him, Sebastian grabbed the book from Constantine's grasp. The vampire toppled to the side. Sebastian shoved the book in Alexa's face.

"What do you think happens now when it's vampire blood spilled on this book?"

She snarled, her face twisting in anger. But under the anger he could smell fear. It wafted from the other vampires as well. They feared the book.

They feared him.

"I'll tell you what happens. I call for the destruction of all the clan heads!" He held the book aloft. Wet blood from the pages dribbled down his wrist. With it, he felt the power in the book surge forth. In his mind's eye, he saw each of the clan heads: Kobol, Tramplain, Jucael, Xavier, and Celine. Each faltered, staggering as they felt the book's effects reach them. Tramplain fell to his knees, blood running from his ears. Celine clung to red velvet curtains, fighting to remain on her feet. Kobol sagged in his throne chair, head in his hands.

Die, all of you die.

But he didn't know the right words to make it happen. Even with the power of the book, he couldn't control it completely without the right words. All he could do was absorb their power, revert them to regular vampires.

No more clan heads and with that, no more organized vampire society. Chaos in the vampire world, which would make them easier to pick off.

Alexa crouched in front of him, lips pulled back from her teeth revealing her sharp fangs. "You think you've won a victory here, Sebastian? You'll pay for it. I'll make sure you pay dearly."

She spun away from him and ran out one of the open doors. The other vampires looked confused, disoriented. Without Constantine to guide them, they weren't sure what to do. They must have been tethered to him longer, unable to function on their own, whereas Alexa had only been a vampire beholden to Constantine for a year.

Finally one of the vampires snarled and backed away toward another of the open doors. The other vampires clustered around him. Then their heads jerked around, as if listening. A moment later Sebastian heard it too. Footsteps, running toward them. Coming from all the doors.

A moment later, In-Between burst into the room. Nigel jumped out from the door nearest the vampires. He yelled and swung with a silver blade. The vampires roared and slashed at him, dodging the knife. Nigel pressed on, causing them to retreat around the table.

From behind them, Jessica appeared. She sprayed them with holy water. The vampires screamed. Steam rose from their exposed flesh. The stench of rotting flesh filled the room, making Sebastian cough. As the vampires writhed and shrieked, the In-Between closed in, dispatching them with swift efficiency. Heads were severed from bodies and stuffed into sacks. The pieces would be dragged to the surface and burned.

Jessica crossed around the table and knelt beside Constantine.

"He's not finished," she said and gestured to one of the In-Between. He stepped forward with an axe and severed Constantine's head.

Across the room, Nigel grabbed Stan by the arm and hauled him to his feet. "What about this guy?"

"Please," Stan said. He covered his face in his hands.

Sebastian stared at him. Thin, quivering body, stringing hair, shoulders hunched in defeat, but he was responsible for countless deaths and could have caused so much more damage.

"He gave the book to Constantine," Sebastian said. "He betrayed Corbin, betrayed us."

Nigel's hand tightened on Stan's arm. "We'll deal with him then."

"No, please. Wait, Sebastian!" Stan's reached out a beseeching hand as several In-Between grabbed him and hauled him out through one of the doors. In a moment, the In-Between were gone, dragging away the vampire corpses, leaving Sebastian and Jessica in the empty room.

"I thought you were in trouble," Sebastian said.

Jessica gave him a slight smile. "I could say the same about you." She gestured at the book. "You found it at least."

"Or it found me," he said. He looked down at it, covered in blood. He could still feel the power of it coursing through his body. In the back of his mind he could hear it whispering to him, promising power, eternal life, dominion over all. So tempting...

"We have to destroy it." Jessica's voice tugged at his attention. He blinked, looking up at her.

"Yes. Ah, yes. Okay."

Her eyes narrowed. "Sebastian, we do have to destroy it. It's too dangerous to leave it."

"You're right, I know you're right." He nodded, his head bobbing up and down.

She reached out a hand. "Give me the book."

He leaned away from her. "Why?"

"Fine. Never mind." She lowered her hand. He relaxed. She darted forward, swiping the book from his hand.

"Hey!" He grabbed for her but she leapt away around the table.

"Come on, give it back," he said. He followed around the table. She kept moving, keeping the table between them.

"Sebastian, the book has to be destroyed. Look at you. You can't even stand to let it out of your hands. Can't you see how dangerous it is?"

"It let me destroy the clan heads," he said. "Maybe I can find a way to stop all the vampires. I just need some time to work that out." He lunged for her. "Give it to me!"

She jumped back, out of his reach. "No way!"

From her back pocket, she pulled out a small bottle of lighter fluid. She squeezed it all over the book. Sebastian shrieked and raced around the table. She dodged him, staying just out of his reach.

He grabbed for her, missing by inches. He could feel the book calling him. He knew he could stop the vampires with it. He just needed a little more time with it, a little more time to figure out its ways. A few carefully spoken words and he could destroy vampirism forever. Couldn't she understand what that meant? It would free them, all of the In-Between. No longer would they be stuck in a half world. They would be free to be normal people again. Couldn't she understand that, the bitch!

"Jessica, give it to me. I can stop the vampires. I know I can. You can destroy it when I'm done."

She shook her head. "Sorry Sebastian, it's already got too much of a hold on you. I can see it." She dropped the lighter fluid and pulled out a lighter.

"No, you bitch!" He lunged one final time.

She flicked the lighter. Flame shot up, licking the pages. The cover began to brown and curl.

Pain slammed into Sebastian. He grabbed his head. Arcs of pain pierced his temples, raced across his skull. He screamed and fell to his knees. The smell of scorched flesh burned in his nostrils, filling his lungs. He choked, coughing, hacking until he almost vomited. Blazing light blinded him. He squeezed his eyes shut but the light still burned. His body jerked and writhed on the floor. His nerves shrieked. His heart thundered in his chest as if it was going to explode out of his chest or maybe just bash itself to bits.

Howling sounded in his ears, speaking gibberish he didn't understand. He would have, he knew, if he'd had more time with the book. But she'd burned it, destroyed it, ruined it, ruined him and his opportunity to fix everything, to get rid of the vampires and claim all the power inherent in their condition. He could have used that power for whatever he wanted. He could have cured the In-Between, he could have helped people, he could have made them do whatever he wanted, he could have forced Alexa to bow down to him, he could have...

His mind snapped, recoiling from the images flooding his brain. *What is that, what is that?* The question echoed in his mind. What were those images? He would never do that, never want that, not in a million years. He couldn't do that, couldn't become a monster worse than any vampire, sucking away people's souls for sustenance. How could he think that?

He couldn't.

But the book could.

The book.

He felt the grip of it loosen on his mind and only then did he realize how much of a grip it had held. How long had it been grasping, directing him? Had it been looking for just the right one, at just the right point on the In-Between continuum? The vampires were too close to hear it properly, the humans too far away, but the In-Between were just close enough, but not every In-Between.

Just a certain one, leaning far enough to being a vampire.

Just him.

His body stopped jerking. He felt hands grabbing his shoulders. His head cradled in a lap. He opened his eyes.

Jessica looked down at him. Tears streaked her face. Her hair stuck up around her hair in a mass of tangles and disarray. He turned his head to look at the pile of smoldering ash on the floor. Funny how there was so much of it for a book.

He must have said something aloud as Jessica answered him.

"It seemed to expand in the fire before it started to burn down," she said. Her hand tightened on his shoulder. "Are you okay?"

He heard the fear in her voice. "Yeah, I'm okay now."

He sat up. She helped him until he sat beside her.

"It's gone now," he said. He looked over at her. "You did the right thing."

Her smile looked thin and strained on her face. "Good."

They both climbed to their feet. He leaned against the table and took one last look at the pile of ash. For a moment, he wanted to kick out at it, spread the ash across the floor but he didn't touch it. Even burned, he didn't want to take the chance.

"Let's get out of here," he said.

She nodded and took his hand to lead him back to the surface.

CHAPTER FIFTEEN

The remaining In-Between insisted on holding services for Corbin and the people who died defending him. Neither Sebastian or Jessica really wanted to go, but Nigel insisted. Joan also said it was a good idea, for both of them, saying something about healing. Sebastian didn't believe in it anymore but when Jessica began to soften her stance, he went to support her.

The ceremony took place at dusk, the best time for most In-Between. Still Sebastian wore sunglasses. His sensitivity had exerted itself with a vengeance again. Even with the darkened lenses, his head pounded until the last rays of the sun faded from the sky. The final speaker finished and the fifteen people in attendance bowed their heads in silence one last time. After a few moments, several people began to drift away toward the house. Sebastian waited for Jessica to move but she didn't. He waited with her until they were the last two outside.

Soothing darkness spread across the land, darkening the trees and covering the fresh graves. The In-Between had dug up the crude holes he and Jessica had made and reburied the bodies farther from the house, in a natural grove surrounded on three sides by trees. Simple stone markers marked each of the graves.

When it got dark enough, Sebastian removed his sunglasses and slipped them into his pocket.

"I heard there are more attacks," Jessica said. "Nigel said it's more random, more frantic."

"They're like wild animals now," he said.

"Easier to pick off too," she said. "They hardly hide any more. Reports are coming in from all over. Some of them forget to hide when the sun comes up. It's weird. It's like..."

"It's like the head has been cut off," he said. "Destroying the clan heads destroyed the intelligence in most of them, probably depending on how long they'd been vampires. The longer they were enslaved to their clan head, the more mindless they are now. The more cunning ones will be the newer vampires."

"Or the clan heads themselves," she said. "Maybe their lost their influence, but they probably didn't lose their own minds."

"I think a couple of them did."

She looked over at him. He could see her frown in the dark.

"How..." she started then shook her head. "I don't want to know."

"This might be a new era with vampires," he said. "We might have a chance of wiping them out."

"As long as we can get the new ones too," she said. "The ones that are still thinking."

"Yeah." A memory tugged at his mind. A lot of what had happened in the underground room was a blur to him now. The destruction of the book had scrambled his memories. Still Stan had corroborated his story, which was enough to earn Stan a lifetime of prison instead of immediate execution by the In-Between.

Now one of those missing memories peaked through the mist in Sebastian's mind. He saw a sneering mouth full of fangs and a familiar pixie cut.

"I'll make sure you pay dearly."

A chill ran through him that had nothing to do with the temperature. He remembered those words, and the voice that had spoken them to him.

Alexa.

Jessica turned to him. Her head tilted. "What is it?"

"I have to go," he said. He turned and headed for the house.

"Go? Where?" She jogged to catch up. She grabbed his arm to stop him. "Where are you going?"

"Home." The word burst out of him. He hadn't even known he was going to say it but it sounded right, it felt right. He had to go home.

"Why?" she said.

He opened his mouth to tell her but the mists in his mind closed again. Why did he feel he had to go home? He knew it had to do with the events in the underground room but he couldn't remember. Still the feeling lingered and grew stronger.

"I don't know," he said. "But I need to go. I know that sounds weird."

She smiled and shook her head. "It's okay. You've been sounding weird practically the whole time I've known you. Don't get all pouty."

"I'm not pouting," he said. "Am I really that weird?"

"You were talking about going home," she said.

"Yes, right. I have to go," he said. "Ah, would you come with me?"

Her grip on his arm tightened. "Try to stop me."

He opened his mouth to reply but her kiss silenced him. Their shadows blended into one in the darkness.

About the Author

Based in Toronto, Canada, Rebecca M. Senese writes horror, science fiction and mystery/crime, often all at once in the same story. Garnering an Honorable Mention in "The Year's Best Science Fiction" and nominated for numerous Aurora Awards, her work has appeared in *Tesseracts 16: Parnassus Unbound*, *Imaginarium 2012*, *Tesseracts 15: A Case of Quite Curious Tales*, *Ride the Moon*, *TransVersions*, *Deadbolt Magazine*, *On Spec*, *The Vampire's Crypt*, *Storyteller*, *Reflection's Edge*, *Future Syndicate* and *Into the Darkness*, amongst others.

When not serving up tales of the macabre, mysterious or wondrous, she volunteers as a zombie or vampire at haunted attractions in October to stalk and scare all the unsuspecting innocents.

Find Me Online

Website - http://www.RebeccaSenese.com
Twitter - http://twitter.com/RebeccaSenese